The Love Game

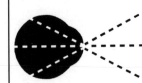

THE ANDERSON FAMILY

THE LOVE GAME

REGINA HART

THORNDIKE PRESS
A part of Gale, Cengage Learning

GALE
CENGAGE Learning·

Farmington Hills, Mich • San Francisco • New York • Waterville, Maine
Meriden, Conn • Mason, Ohio • Chicago

GALE
CENGAGE Learning

LIBRARY OF CONGRESS CATALOGING-IN-PUBLICATION DATA

Hart, Regina.
  The love game / by Regina Hart. — Large print edition.
    pages cm. — (Thorndike Press large print African-American) (The Anderson family ; #1)
    ISBN 978-1-4104-8286-0 (hardcover) — ISBN 1-4104-8286-3 (hardcover)
    1. African Americans—Fiction. 2. Video games industry—Fiction. 3. Large type books. I. Title.
PS3608.A7867L68 2015
813'.6—dc23   2015021423

Published in 2015 by arrangement with Harlequin Books S.A.

Printed in Mexico
1 2 3 4 5 6 7 19 18 17 16 15

Dear Reader,

Several Christmases ago, my husband gifted me with The Supremes' *Greatest Hits* CD. I love The Supremes, don't you? Listening to their songs over and over — and over — that Christmas, I heard three distinct heroines: one who's open to love ("I Hear a Symphony"), one who's jaded ("Nothing but Heartaches") and one who's too busy for love ("Stoned Love"). At least that's my interpretation. For years, I've wanted to tell their stories. Today, I can finally introduce you to the Beharie sisters.

In *The Love Game,* Iris is looking for love. However, she doesn't realize love comes in its own time, which isn't always convenient. In fact, it's often complicated. I hope you enjoy Iris and Tyler. Meanwhile, I'm having fun writing Rose's story. Rose has given up on love — but love won't give up on Rose.

Enjoy!

Regina

To my dream team:
My sister, Bernadette, for giving me
the dream
My husband, Michael, for supporting
the dream
My brother Richard for believing in
the dream
My brother Gideon for encouraging
the dream
And to Mom and Dad always with love.

ACKNOWLEDGMENTS

Many thanks to Chris T., network analyst, for his help with the technology details. I apologize for any misinterpretations I may have made.

CHAPTER 1

"You're not ready to take charge."

Tyler Anderson had heard those words from his father before. In the past, he'd been disappointed and hurt. But this time, Foster Anderson's certainty that Tyler wasn't ready to lead their family-owned computer gaming company fired him up.

"I disagree." He locked gazes with his father, who was also his boss.

"All right." Foster settled back on his chair. A spark of interest brightened the ebony eyes Tyler had inherited. "Convince me."

"I've worked at Anderson Adventures for more than twenty years, since I was fifteen." Tyler straightened, laying out his case with confidence. "I've been around these offices, watching and learning what everyone does since I was eight. I know this company from the bottom up."

"That's true." Foster nodded. "You know

the company's operations."

"I've shadowed key people in every department — finance, sales, human resources, information technology, customer service."

His father was aware of the finance classes Tyler had taken. But no one could see the numbers as clearly as his cousin, Xavier Anderson, the company's vice president of finance. Foster also knew Tyler had made sales calls with Donovan Carroll, his college classmate and Anderson Adventures' vice president of sales.

"I don't dispute that you know this company almost as well as I do." Foster balanced his elbows on the arms of his black leather chair, locking his fingers together in front of his pale gray shirt. "Son, you know how proud I've always been of your interest in the company. But Anderson Adventures is more than its departments."

"As vice president of product development, I'm aware of that." Tyler leaned forward as he rushed to reassure his father. "I've designed several of our most successful games."

"You've designed all of them. You have a keen imagination, as well as great creative talent and programming skills. You've built a very fine product-development depart-ment."

"Then why don't you think I'm ready to lead the company?" Tyler's head was spin-ning. *What am I missing?*

Foster's sigh came from deep inside. "I've explained this to you before. Anderson Adventures is more than the computer games we develop. I don't question that you know enough about the operation to run the business. What I question is whether you have the people skills to lead the company."

Foster rose from his chair and strolled to the window, sliding his hands into the front pockets of his slate-gray suit pants. Tyler's father was a tall, lean, charismatic figure. Despite his quiet demeanor, people knew when he entered a room. Foster's sepia-brown chiseled face was smooth and clean shaven. His tight curls were still dark brown with barely a hint of gray. Physically fit, Foster exercised at least five days a week. Tyler often jogged with him on the weekends and was sore by Monday morn-ing, just as he was today.

"I don't understand." Tyler stared at his father, trying to read the older man's mind. "If you think I can run the business, why don't you think I can lead the company?"

Foster turned from his fifth-floor view of

downtown Columbus, Ohio. It was the first Monday of March. Still, the threat of snow hung heavy in the clouds. "Did you know Jonas in accounting has a son who earned his master's from Clemson University last semester?"

"No, I didn't."

"The company sent his son a gift card as a graduation present."

"That's nice." *But what does it have to do with my running the company?* "Last month, Trudy in purchasing became a grandmother for the third time. Her daughter delivered a healthy baby boy."

"That's wonderful." *Why are you telling me this?*

"The company sent flowers to her daughter's hospital room." Foster cocked his head. "You didn't know that, either, did you?"

"No, I didn't." *And your point is . . . ?*

Foster crossed back to his desk, past the row of photos on his wall. Here, images of holiday potlucks, birthday festivities, engagement parties and baby showers memorialized Anderson Adventures' celebrations. His father settled back onto his chair. "When was the last time you spoke to your coworkers, other than Xavier and Donovan?"

Does saying hello when I pass people in the hallway, cafeteria or restroom count? Probably not.

"I . . ." Tyler's gaze shifted to the family photos lining the credenza behind his father's desk. There was one of him and his father with Tyler's mother, taken the last year of her life.

"You know the business side of Anderson Adventures but you don't know its people." Foster took a drink of coffee from the World's Greatest Dad mug Tyler had given him when he was nine years old. "And the fact is, it's the people behind the company who've made it a success."

"I know."

Foster gave him a dubious look. "You need to work harder to show it, son."

"I will."

"Good, because I've decided to retire at the end of this year."

"What?" Shock and apprehension sent a chill through Tyler's nervous system. "Why?"

Foster chuckled. "I'm sixty-eight years old, Ty. This company has consumed more than half of my life. It's been fun, exciting, frustrating and challenging. Now I'm tired. It's time for me to move aside and let younger people — you, Xavier and Donovan — take the reins."

Now Tyler was apprehensive for another reason. "Xavier and Van aren't interested in running the company. They've said as much."

"I know. But your taking over as CEO is not guaranteed, son." Foster leveled a look at him.

"If not me, then who?"

"I'd have to go outside of the company." Foster's eyes were troubled.

Silence crashed into his father's office. Tyler took a moment to pull his thoughts together. "Anderson Adventures is a family-owned company. You'd hire an outsider to lead it?"

"I don't want to but I will if I have to."

Tyler rubbed his eyes with his thumb and two fingers. "Dad, I've got to tell you, I'm not happy with the idea of a stranger taking over our company. Xavier and Van won't be, either."

"Then don't let it happen." Foster brooked no argument. "Step away from your computer. Prove you can run this business *and* lead its people."

"How am I supposed to do that?" Frustration tightened the muscles in Tyler's neck and shoulders even as he strained to keep it from his voice.

"We're releasing your latest computer game in July."

"Right." Tyler nodded. " 'Osiris's Journey.' We're dropping it simultaneously online and through brick-and-mortar stores the weekend after Independence Day."

"You're going to hire a marketing consultant and be the point person for our product launch. You'll have to work with our accountants to manage the budget, our sales team to come up with the list of key accounts, and our IT team for testing and talking points."

"I'm vice president of a department." Tyler struggled to mask his horror. "I can't tie up my time on a product launch." Not to mention the fact he didn't want to interact with that many people.

"Learn to delegate." Foster lifted a business card from his desk. "And I want you to interview The Beharie Agency."

"I've never heard of them." Tyler took the card from his father.

"It's an up-and-coming firm. I know the family and I have it on good authority that the agency is creative, professional and customer focused."

"I'll give them a call." Tyler rose to leave.

"I want you to succeed, son." Foster's words stopped him. "But if you don't have

17

loyalty from the people in the company, the company won't succeed."

Tyler nodded, then exited his father's office. He felt the weight of Foster's words — as well as incredible pressure. He had less than four months to gain the loyalty of Anderson Adventures' seventy employees — not including himself, and his father, aunt, cousin and college classmate.

What if I fail?

Then the forty-three-year-old company founded by his father and uncle would be turned over to a stranger. He couldn't let that happen.

Tyler glanced at the business card in his hand: Iris Beharie, President, The Beharie Agency.

Can you help me with the most important product launch of my life?

Tuesday morning, Iris Beharie pushed through the glass doors leading to the fifth-floor reception area of Anderson Adventures. She scanned the room, half expecting to be pounced on by a television crew, telling her she'd been punked. How would a multimillion-dollar company know about her little firm and why would they invite her to submit a bid for their product launch? If they didn't have their own in-house marketing and public relations department, then surely they had a much larger marketing consultant company on retainer.

The friendly woman at the modern and modular front reception desk who'd buzzed her in regarded her with a curious smile. "Good morning. May I help you?"

Iris surreptitiously wiped her sweaty palm on the skirt of her cream business suit. She stepped forward. "Good morning. I'm Iris Beharie. I have a nine o'clock appointment with Tyler Anderson."

With her pretty, wholesome looks; neat, blond bob; and twinkling, cornflower-blue eyes, the receptionist reminded Iris of an older Doris Day. Her nameplate read Sherry Parks.

"Just a moment." Sherry picked up the telephone receiver and selected a few buttons. "Ty, Iris Beharie is here to see you." Pause. "All right." She stood as she replaced the phone, then gestured toward the crimson leather guest chairs beside her desk. "He'll be with you in a few minutes. Please make yourself comfortable. May I take your coat?"

"Thank you." Iris handed over her periwinkle wool coat. She kept her briefcase with her.

Sherry walked to a section of the cherry-wood wall and slid it open to reveal a closet. The receptionist hung Iris's coat, then slid the door closed again. "Would you like some coffee?"

"I'd love some, if it isn't any trouble."

Sherry waved a dismissive hand. "It's no trouble at all. Cream and sugar?"

"Just cream. Thank you."

Sherry's brisk pace carried her past other administrative desks and into a back room.

Iris turned toward the crimson guest chairs. The two-inch heels of her cream pumps were silent on the thick silver-and-black carpet. Despite its cool glass-and-metal decor, the reception area gave the impression of warmth and welcome. It also was well-maintained. Her eyes skimmed the covers of the industry magazines neatly spread across the tempered glass Caravan desk in the far corner.

The walls showcased their most successful games, as well as candid metal-framed photos of employees smiling or laughing into the camera. Iris found herself smiling back. Some of the photos had been taken decades earlier, judging by the hair and clothing of the people in the pictures, including a much younger Sherry Parks.

Were Anderson Adventures employees

really that happy? Perhaps if she'd worked for a company like this one, she wouldn't have left her job to start her own firm on a leap of faith.

"I'm sorry I took so long." Sherry reappeared with what looked to be a twenty-ounce mug of coffee.

"Not at all. I appreciate your trouble." Iris took the hot drink from the receptionist. "This is one big mug."

"The Andersons love their coffee. And they assume everyone else does, too." Sherry returned to her desk.

The fondness in the woman's voice implied a positive employee morale. A good sign.

Iris settled onto one of the guest chairs. "That's a lot of pressure on whoever makes the coffee."

"Whoever gets here first makes it. That's usually Foster, Tyler, Xavier or Donovan." Sherry settled onto her chair, pulling it under the desk. "After that, whoever pours the last cup makes the next pot."

Very egalitarian. It was a credit to these high-powered executives that they didn't wait for the staff to make the coffee. And the fact that Tyler Anderson — the vice president of product development — regularly arrived at work early enough to make the first pot explained how he could have responded so early Monday morning to the proposal she'd submitted Sunday night.

Iris took a sip. "This is delicious. Who made it?"

"If it's good, it wasn't Van. Everyone complains his coffee tastes like antifreeze. He says, if they don't like it, they should get in earlier." Sherry paused as they both laughed. "But the coffee goes pretty quickly. It's nine o'clock. That's probably the third pot."

Iris's eyes widened. "You weren't kidding about their coffee addiction."

"Sorry to keep you waiting." A strong baritone resonated throughout Iris's nervous system. "Ty Anderson."

Iris looked up — way up — to the tall, dark, handsome man who'd stopped in front of her. *This* was the vice president of product development? She was definitely being played. The only way a desk jockey would look like Idris Elba was if he came from central casting.

His features were silver-screen perfect. His high forehead and bright ebony eyes indicated a keen intelligence that one shouldn't underestimate. His squared jaw signaled a stubbornness that would be a challenge. His full, well-shaped lips implied a subtle sensuality she shouldn't even think about.

Iris stood, taking his large, outstretched hand. His warm skin sent a shock up her arm. "It's nice to meet you, Mr. Anderson. I'm Iris Beharie."

"Ty. This way, please." He stepped aside, releasing her hand to gesture in the direction from which he'd come. "Sherry, thank you."

"You're welcome, Ty." The Doris Day double gave him a fond look.

Iris settled the strap of her black briefcase onto her left shoulder and hoisted the mammoth coffee mug with her right hand. "Thank you."

"You're welcome." Sherry lifted her hands, crossing her fingers. "Good luck."

Iris tossed Sherry a grateful smile before following Tyler down the hall. His broad shoulders were wrapped in a white jersey. His long legs were covered in chocolate suit pants. She jerked her gaze from his butt and looked around the office suite. Tyler stopped beside a frosted glass door and waved her inside. She glimpsed his name and title on the silver frame beside the threshold.

"Have a seat." He closed his door, then waited for Iris to claim a chair at the small glass conversation table.

"Thank you." Her palms were sweating again.

His office was big, bright and painfully neat. Project folders were staggered in a metal filing system on his silver-and-glass L-shaped desk. His black leather chair was tucked under his table. One of the twenty-ounce silver-and-black coffee mugs stood beside his computer mouse.

Her office would drive him nuts.

Tyler also seemed obsessed with time. His large desk calendar was covered with notes. Dates were crossed off the wall calendar opposite his desk. Project timelines were pinned to a board behind his chair.

Frightening.

Iris noted his minifridge, microwave and radio. Was he preparing for a lockdown?

Tyler came around to join her at the conversation table. Rather than watch him fold his long, lean body onto the smoke-gray padded seat opposite her, Iris distracted herself by pulling a writing tablet and pen from her briefcase.

"Your proposal is impressive." Tyler tapped the electronic tablet in front of him.

"Thank you." So far, so good.

"I've also reviewed your firm's website. The two seem to be in contradiction."

"How so?" Iris gripped her ballpoint pen as she forced herself to hold Tyler's penetrating gaze. She really wanted this account.

"You're a one-person show. How can one person accomplish all the things you've promised in your proposal?"

"I understand your concern." She'd heard it before from other executives. "However, I assure you I wouldn't have made those commitments if I wasn't confident I'd be able to meet them."

"How?"

Iris glanced at the tablet trapped between the table and the long, elegant fingers of Tyler's right hand. "As I explained in my proposal, this isn't my first product launch. I know what's involved. That experience will make me more efficient with your project."

"You also mentioned other consultants you plan to work with." Tyler leaned back on his seat.

"Their costs are included in the budget."

"You, a designer, a printer and a media buyer. That's a lot of people to depend on to meet deadlines."

Iris put down her pen, then rested one hand on top of the other. "That's a legitimate concern. But, Mr. Anderson —"

"Ty. Mr. Anderson is my father."

"Ty." Iris inclined her head with a smile.

"Even if you worked with a larger company, you'd still need those various roles. The only difference between my firm and a larger company is that those responsibilities would be assigned to their staff. But you'd still have to depend on a lot of people meeting their deadlines."

Tyler's mind wandered as he watched Iris's full, bow-shaped lips. It was only when her lips stopped moving that he realized he should have been listening.

He tamped down his embarrassment — and his urge to trace a finger over her lips. "That's a lot of people to keep track of during the project. We don't have a lot of time."

"This launch does have an ambitious schedule. This is the second week of March and your release date is July tenth."

"That's just over four months." Tyler scowled. *Why haven't I heard from Peter Kimball about his company's proposal?*

"Seventeen weeks and three days. It's a tight schedule, but not impossible." Iris spread her small, delicate hands. The movement briefly distracted Tyler.

"You've worked with tough deadlines before?"

Iris sat back and crossed her legs. "Many times and always successfully."

Her voice was matter-of-fact, her manner

26

confident. Her proposal was impressive in its detail and vision. Still, Tyler hesitated.

This was a big job. Iris Beharie had more than eight years of marketing and public relations experience. However, the results of his internet research indicated The Beharie Agency was only three months old. How could he entrust his launch of his company's new computer game to what amounted to an untried agency?

How could he trust her with his future?

Tyler hardened his heart to her honey-brown skin although it looked as soft as silk. He pulled his gaze from warm, coffee eyes that threatened to brainwash him. Her subtle citrus fragrance would haunt his dreams tonight.

He picked up his tablet and stared blankly at her proposal. *Just say no, thank her for coming and call Peter Kimball — for the fifth time.* "Your proposal is good."

"You read my website." Her voice was strained. "You saw the list of other projects I've completed."

"You were with another company when you did that work." Tyler was snared by her gaze again.

"I don't have a large company behind me, but I do have an experienced and talented network of professional associates with whom I've worked before."

Tyler dragged his finger across the tablet's screen to flip through Iris's proposal again. He'd practically committed it to memory: pricing, tasks, goals, detailed launch schedule. Could she pull it off? There was too much at stake to take the risk.

He lowered the tablet. "I'll consider what we've discussed, then call you with my decision."

Iris gave him a rueful smile. "Let's be honest, Ty. You're not going to hire me, are you?"

Tyler hesitated but he couldn't bring himself to lie. "No, I'm afraid not. I'm sorry."

"So am I." Iris sighed. She repacked her pen and notepad before standing.

Tyler stood with her. "Your proposal was really very good. In fact, it was great."

"But you don't have confidence in my execution." Her words were blunt but her tone wasn't accusatory.

"There's a lot riding on this product launch." Now that their meeting was over, Tyler didn't want her to leave.

"Every launch is important." She adjusted her briefcase strap on her slender shoulder, then offered him her hand. "Good luck with your launch."

"Thanks." Tyler took her hand, surprised by her gesture. *Why wasn't she being snide or sarcastic like other companies usually were when he turned down their proposal?* "Good luck with your company."

"Thank you." Iris led him to his office door.

Their conversation was scarce as they walked down the hallway: the weather, traffic and the hard winter they'd just had.

They stopped beside Sherry's desk. Tyler offered Iris his hand again, one last time to feel her soft, warm skin against his. "Thanks again for meeting with me."

"Thank you for the opportunity." Her smile wasn't as bright as it had been when they'd first met but it was sincere. She slipped her hand from Tyler's, then turned to Sherry. "It was nice to meet you, Sherry."

The receptionist smiled up at her. "Same here, dear. Have a good day."

"You do the same." Iris pushed through the glass doors of the office suite, then disappeared down the hall to the elevator.

Tyler sensed Sherry's eyes on him as he returned to his office. He was certain he'd made the right decision regarding The Beharie Agency. Then why was he having second thoughts? Was it because of the undeniable strength of Iris's proposal?

Or her full bow-shaped lips?

He tried to push thoughts of Iris from his mind as he settled behind his desk to call Kimball & Associates — again. He needed to partner with an established consultant, one they'd worked with before and on whom he could depend to produce a winning launch.

Even if it meant saying no to the opportunity to spend more time in the company of Iris Beharie.

CHAPTER 2

"I need a big account to land a big account or for someone to give me a chance."

Iris trailed her friend Cathy Yee through the buffet line during the monthly Marketing Professionals Association luncheon Tuesday afternoon. The group had taken over a banquet room in one of the downtown restaurants. Well-dressed marketing professionals on an extended lunch break packed the dim walnut-wood room. Circular tables covered in white cloths faced the speaker's podium. Serving stations lined the far walls of the cramped space.

Iris considered the menu items: potato or chicken-noodle soup, green or pasta salad, turkey or veggie wrap, coffee or water, chocolate chip cookie or fudge brownie. She skipped the salads, and stuck to the meat selections, coffee and both dessert choices.

"I know. I was there once." Cathy, a freelance designer who'd been flying solo for almost ten years, passed on the soups, but chose both salads, both wraps, coffee, two fudge brownies and a cookie.

Iris considered her friend's waiflike, five-foot-two-inch frame clothed in a black pantsuit with onyx accessories. Where would all that food go?

"I was so disappointed not to get that contract with Anderson Adventures." Iris balanced her lunch plate and bowl in one hand, and her coffee cup in another. "It's as though the three months I've spent in my own business has completely wiped out my eight years of experience."

Iris frowned as her friend led her to a table toward the back of the banquet room. Cathy usually preferred to sit front and center. Maybe she wasn't as interested in this afternoon's social media topic.

"They make you prove yourself all over again." Cathy's voice held more than a touch of irritation.

"Exactly." Iris laid her plate, soup bowl and coffee cup on the empty table Cathy had claimed. The benefits of arriving early.

She and Cathy had met during one of these lunches years ago. They'd become fast friends. Then when Iris had confided in Cathy about the problems she was dealing with at work, Cathy had encouraged her to strike out on her own. The two partnered on many of their projects. Iris's writing skills allowed Cathy to expand her client services and Cathy provided design work for Iris's contracts.

"It's a good thing you didn't tell your sisters about the interview." Cathy's jaw-length curtain of raven hair swung forward as she pulled her chair under the table.

That would've been bad. "I wanted to land the account before I said anything to them." Iris added cream to her coffee. "Now I don't have to explain that my potential client thinks all of my experience leaked out of my brain when I opened my own firm."

"It would've just given them more ammunition to push you back into working for someone else."

Iris hummed her agreement as she sipped her coffee. "So what's on your mind?"

"What do you mean?" Cathy sounded distracted. Another sign something was bothering her friend.

Iris pointed her fork toward Cathy's plate. "You've piled enough carbs and processed sugar on your plate to put you in a coma. Are you still thinking of returning to the wonderful world of corporate dysfunction?"

Cathy blew a frustrated breath. "The economic recovery is slow and my bills are high. Everything's gone up."

"I understand but just give it a while longer, Cat. Don't give up on your business yet," Iris encouraged her friend, thinking she should take her own advice.

"It's not just the economy." Cathy's words sped up as her annoyance kicked in. "Clients don't want to pay what we're worth. They think since their son has a Mac, why should they pay you to design a brochure when he can do it for free? Or their daughter can spell so why should they pay a professional copywriter?"

"The insane asylum where I used to work had started squeezing vendors that way."

"And what's worse is that these kids, fresh out of college and in many cases untrained, accept this pocket change as their wages instead of researching the industry pay standard." Cathy's voice tightened. "It's insulting."

Iris frowned at her turkey wrap. "Yes, it is. Have you considered your sister's suggestion that you apply to be an adjunct graphic arts professor with her university? It could supplement your business income."

"I'm considering it." Cathy huffed another breath. "I'm not getting any younger, Iris. I've got to —"

"Afternoon, ladies. Mind if we join you?"

The male voice interrupted their conversation.

Iris's heart sank at Peter Kimball's request that he and his associate sit at their table. She gritted a smile and lied through her teeth. "Not at all."

The seasoned marketing professional and owner of Kimball & Associates sat beside her. His young sidekick, a man Iris didn't recognize, took the chair to Peter's left.

Iris sucked in her breath as Peter extended his hand across her chest to Cathy.

"Pete Kimball." The marketing executive gave the designer a toothy smile that didn't reach his pale blue eyes.

"We've met. Cathy Yee." Her friend barely acknowledged him before returning to her veggie wrap.

Peter withdrew his hand, smoothing it over his salt-and-pepper, salon-styled hair. "Oh, yes. You look different. So, Iris, how have you been?"

"Fine, thank you." The waves of irritation Cathy generated distracted Iris.

"I heard you left RGB." Peter dug into his pasta salad.

"Yes, four months ago." She toyed with her chicken-noodle soup.

"I've always admired your talent. I'm sure I can find a place for you on my team."

35

"Thank you but I'm not looking." Iris suppressed a shudder as she took in his smarmy smile. She considered his deep, golden skin. Was he using a tanning bed? Perhaps that tint came from a can.

Iris glanced at Peter's associate. The young man was methodically making his way across his plate.

"What are you doing, then?" Peter's smile faded as his gaze sharpened.

"I've opened my own marketing and public relations consulting firm, The Beharie Agency."

"Really?" Laughter burst from Peter's throat. "Starting your own business is a lot of hard work. You don't have the exp—"

"I'm ready for more coffee." Cathy nudged her. "Want some?"

Iris looked at her still full cup. "Yes."

She joined Cathy, leaving the table without excusing herself.

"What a jackass," Cathy hissed. "He introduces himself to me every time he comes to this thing. How many Chinese women does he know in Columbus, Ohio, that he can't remember me?"

"Consider the source." Iris was offended on her friend's behalf. Peter's laughing in her face when she announced she'd started her own firm didn't seem so bad in comparison. "I can't go back to that table with him."

"We'll find another table."

"But I left my lunch at that one." And she was starting to get hungry.

"Fix yourself another plate." Cathy led them back to the buffet line. "Now we have even more incentive to succeed. You know what they say."

"Living well is the best revenge."

Iris looked forward to proving to Kimball & Associates, as well as Anderson Adventures, that they'd underestimated her. She just needed a chance.

Wednesday was a long day that included participating in a client conference call and drafting another project proposal, which Iris hoped to submit by the end of the week. But tonight she set those thoughts aside as she pulled her canary-yellow Camry into the driveway of her family home. She parked beside her sister Rose's cobalt-blue BMW. Iris was a few minutes early for their weekly family dinner. But as usual, her older sister was already here.

Their dinner was a family tradition Iris and her sisters had continued even after their parents had died. Lily, the middle sister, had moved back into the large suburban home.

Iris grabbed the cake box from the passenger seat. Juggling the box and her purse, she slammed the driver's-side door shut with a hip and pressed the automatic lock button on her key chain. She hurried up the walkway and stairs, then let herself in through the front door.

"Something smells wonderful." Iris followed the scent of seasoned chicken and vegetables down the hallway and into the kitchen.

Rose and Lily stopped talking when she appeared in the doorway. *Paranoid much?*

"You brought dessert." Lily broke the short silence.

"Chocolate cake." Iris sauntered into the kitchen and put the box on the counter beside the stove. She turned to her sisters with her hands on the hips of her powder-blue jeans. "Okay. Let's have it."

"Let's not." Lily continued stirring the pot of chicken stew. Her curvy five-foot-three-inch frame was clothed in faded blue jeans and a bright orange sweatshirt featuring the logo of the Cincinnati's NFL team. Her dark brown hair was a riot of curls that fell past her shoulders.

"Why not?" Rose crossed her arms over her bloodred sweater. With her sleek dark brown hair swinging above her narrow shoulders and her honey-brown features subtly made up, Iris's thirty-four-year-old sister looked more like a runway model than an attorney.

"Because I've gone to a lot of trouble to cook this dinner and I don't want it ruined with an argument." Lily's attention remained on her stew.

Iris arched a brow at Rose. "Does it have to be an argument?"

Lily answered. "No, it doesn't. But lately the two of you can't even agree on the weather."

"That's not a recent development." Iris's tone was dry. "Rose and I have never agreed on anything, especially since she thinks she knows everything."

"Here we go." Lily shook her head as she turned off the burner under the stew.

Rose uncrossed her arms and straightened from the counter. The two-inch heels of her black boots added to her five-foot-eight-inch height. "Maybe if you stopped to consider my advice instead of ignoring it to charge full-speed ahead, you'd realize that sometimes I do know what I'm talking about."

"And *I* know what I'm doing." Iris

dropped her arms. "Why can't you accept that?"

"You *think* you know what you're doing but I'm not so sure." Rose's expression was heavy on the irritation but tempered with concern. "Why did you leave a perfectly good job with a stable company to start a business during a horrible economic climate?"

Cupboards opened and shut as Lily began serving dinner.

Iris arched a brow. "Because it was obvious I wasn't going to advance there."

"At least you had a steady income." Rose threw up her arms. "You could pay your bills. You had health insurance, life insurance, a retirement account and sick days. You won't be able to stay home when you're sick now."

"I rarely used my sick days when I had them."

"Here." Lily forced a soup bowl into Rose's hands, then crossed back to the counter.

"But at least you had them." Rose remained focused on Iris.

"That's fine for you to say." Iris gestured toward her sister. "People at your company respect you and your experience."

"You have to pay your dues, Iris."

"Pay my dues?" Her head was going to pop off her neck. "I'd been with RGB for six years. Meanwhile, new employees were coming in without my experience and leapfrogging over me up the corporate ladder, getting more money and more seniority, while I was doing all the work."

"So you bit off your nose to spite your face."

"What are you talking about?" *Is Rose even hearing me?*

"Rather than stay and fight, you jeopardized your career and your financial security. Meanwhile, the people you were trying to get even with will be fine."

"This isn't about revenge."

"Are you sure?"

"I'd been fighting for six years, Rose." Iris crossed her arms. "It was clear I wasn't going to win that war."

"Here." Lily shoved the stew at Iris.

Iris took the bowl. "What are you doing?"

"I'm going to eat my dinner in peace." Lily carried her stew and ice water toward the dining room.

"You're just going to leave us?" Iris frowned at Lily's back.

Her middle sister turned to face her. "Do you think it's fun for me, listening to the two of you argue all the time? Why do we have these family dinners if it's not to enjoy what's left of our family?"

Iris glanced at Rose. "I —"

"It's just us." Lily sounded tired. "Dad's been dead almost three years. Mom died less than a year ago. I'm in this house, surrounded by happy memories of our past. Then you two come in and shout them down. I don't want to do this anymore. I'm not going to do this anymore. Eat your food, then leave."

Iris's skin heated with shame as Lily walked away. "She seems pissed."

"Yes, she does."

"She never gets pissed."

"No, she doesn't." Rose sighed. "And she's right. We're lucky to have each other. We shouldn't forget that."

Iris nodded. "We should apologize to her."

"Let's do it."

Iris squared her shoulders, then led the way into the dining room. Lily sat alone at the table set for three. Iris took the seat at the place setting across from her. Rose settled beside Iris. Lily ignored them.

Iris waited a beat. "I'm so sorry, Lil."

"So am I." Rose's voice was soft, contrite.

Lily looked up. Iris held her breath, waiting for her sister's response. Lily was the only one who even tried to understand Iris's feelings. She'd never meant to repay her sister's love and support with pain.

Lily spooned more stew. "So how was everybody's day?"

Their laughter shattered the tension. Hours flew by as the sisters enjoyed dinner with seconds and dessert, and good conversation. They shared kitchen duty after the meal. Then Rose and Iris left. The outdoor lights illuminated the porch and driveway. Iris stood on the other side of the front door and listened as Lily connected the locks.

She joined Rose on the driveway. "Be careful driving home."

"You do the same." Rose paused beside Iris's Camry. "Listen, if you decide to go back to work, I'm sure I can help you get a position with another company. I have connections in the business community."

"I *am* working." Iris struggled to keep a hold on her temper.

Rose held up her hands. "You know what I mean."

"Yes, Rosie, I'm afraid I do." *Why are we forever at odds?* "I appreciate your offer. But I don't need my family's help to get a job. I can do this on my own."

"Iris —" Rose stopped herself. She exhaled a familiar, frustrated sigh, then started over. "I know you want to do this by yourself and I commend you. But promise me that, if things get too hard to handle on your own, you'll come to Lil or me for help."

"I promise." But she wouldn't need help. She was going to succeed on her own. She could do this. If only she could land a big enough account.

"Earth to Ty. Are you in here?"

Tyler glanced around at the sound of his cousin's voice. Xavier Anderson, the company's vice president of finance, strode into Tyler's office Thursday afternoon. Donovan Carroll, their friend and vice president of sales, joined him.

"What?" Tyler was still clearing his thoughts from the computer programming problem that bedeviled him.

"We knocked three times." Donovan jerked his clean-shaven brown head toward the door behind him.

Tyler followed the gesture, then returned his attention to the two men. They were both tall and fit, and similarly dressed in dark pants and long-sleeved jerseys.

"I didn't hear you." Tyler pressed a couple of keys to save his computer file.

"That much was obvious." Donovan shoved his hands in the pockets of his gray

Dockers. "We should assign someone to check on you in case of a fire. I'm sure you wouldn't hear the alarm."

"Van and I are going to lunch." Xavier stopped behind a guest chair. "Do you want to join us?"

"No, thanks. I packed." Besides, Lauren Cobb, Xavier's girlfriend of two months, would probably be there. He'd rather eat alone.

"You're going to make me be the third wheel?" Donovan sounded as though he was only half joking.

"Sorry, man." Tyler gave him a sympathetic look.

"You need to get out of your office once in a while, Ty." Donovan pulled his hands from his pockets and folded himself onto one of the two gray guest chairs opposite Tyler's desk.

Xavier took the other. "Have you heard from Kimball & Associates?"

"No, I haven't." Tyler looked at his black Movado watch. It was almost noon. "I thought you were going to lunch."

"We have a few minutes." Donovan shrugged. "So what's the status on Kimball?"

Tyler turned away from his computer. Obviously, they weren't going to let him get back to work. "They haven't acknowledged my request for a proposal. They haven't even responded to my emails or returned my calls."

Xavier blew out a breath, sounding almost as disgusted as Tyler felt. "We've been working with them for years. Why are they now giving us poor service?"

Donovan glanced at Xavier. "I heard a couple of their account representatives recently left the company."

Xavier ran a hand over his close-cropped hair. "You're going to have to go with the other company."

"You know I can't do that." Tyler leaned back on his chair. "This is our summer product launch. It needs to carry us into the fall. Iris Beharie's a solo operation. One person can't handle a project this big."

The other men knew what was at stake. He'd told them. If he didn't put together a successful product launch, Foster would name a chief executive officer from outside of the family. He couldn't allow that to happen on his watch.

"It's March nineteenth." Donovan shook his head. " 'Osiris's Journey' drops July tenth. We only have sixteen weeks before the release."

"I know the schedule." Tyler rubbed his

eyes with his thumb and two fingers. "I've found a couple of other companies to contact."

"We don't have time, Ty." Xavier pinned him with his onyx stare. "You're going to have to go with The Beharie Agency."

Tyler frowned at the other two company vice presidents. He hated not being in control and that's what had just happened. He'd gambled on hearing from the larger company. But the clock had run out, leaving him in the risky position of having to work with Iris Beharie. The threat came on two fronts. Professionally, Tyler wasn't confident Iris could deliver a successful launch, which he needed to ensure Anderson Adventures remained in his family's control. Personally, he didn't know whether he'd be able to resist his attraction to the marketing professional. He didn't know whether he'd want to.

Tyler sighed. "I just need another week."

"Why are you resisting working with The Beharie Agency?" Xavier gave him the penetrating stare that made Tyler think his cousin could read his mind. "You were impressed with her proposal. Van and I read it, and we agreed with you."

Donovan nodded. "It was detailed, creative and unique to our company. So what's wrong?"

There was too much at risk. "Suppose halfway through the project, she's unable to meet her contractual obligations?"

"We'll deal with it — if it comes to that." Donovan spread his hands.

"If it came to that, it would be too late." Strain made Tyler's voice brittle.

"You don't have to prove yourself to us." Xavier broke the momentary silence. "We know you're a genius when it comes to game design and programming. And you know everything there is to know about this company."

"That's not good enough for my father." The words were even harder to admit today. Would he be able to reach the bar his father had set for him?

"Foster wants you to spend more time getting to know our associates. And he's right." Xavier's casual shrug belied the intense look in his eyes.

"What am I supposed to do?" Tyler jerked his chin toward the frosted-glass door of his office. "Walk up and down the hallways, asking people how their day's going?"

"That's what I do." Donovan's hazel-brown eyes twinkled with irreverent humor.

"You do a lot of things I wouldn't do." For example, agreeing to share a meal with

Lauren Cobb.

"Then maybe Foster's right." Xavier frowned. "Despite your programming genius, your design creativity, the decades you've spent learning every aspect of the company, maybe you aren't the right person to lead Anderson Adventures. If the only thing standing in the way of your goal is getting to know the people who actually keep the company going, Foster *is* better off looking outside for his successor."

The rebuke stung, just as Xavier had meant it to. "Why does he have to look outside of the company? Why can't you or Van take over?"

"That's a good question. Why can't you ascend to the throne, Xavier?" Lauren Cobb's amused voice preceded her into the room.

At her entrance, Tyler stood with his cousin and his friend. *What is it about her that makes me want to leave my own office?*

Xavier kissed her cheek. "I thought you were going to meet us in the reception area."

"You kept me waiting." There was a light scolding in her reply. "I had to come looking for you. I wasn't going to wait with the receptionist."

An image of Iris Beharie laughing with Sherry formed in Tyler's mind. They'd seemed to enjoy each other's company after only a few minutes. Even following their disappointing meeting, Iris had smiled at Sherry and called her by name as she'd left their offices. In contrast, Lauren had met Xavier for lunch several times a week for months. Did she know Sherry's name wasn't The Receptionist? In fact, Sherry's name was on a wooden plaque that sat on her desk. Had Lauren bothered to notice it?

Xavier took Lauren's hand. "Then let's go. I invited Van to join us."

"Oh." Lauren glanced at Donovan before returning her gaze to Xavier.

Donovan exchanged a silent question with Tyler, who shrugged. Why would his friend have agreed to join the couple for lunch? Xavier must not have been completely forthcoming with his invitation.

His cousin arched a brow at him. "Are you sure you won't join us?"

Positive. "Thanks anyway."

Lauren put her free hand on Xavier's chest. "I'm still waiting for my answer. Why can't you take over Anderson Adventures when your uncle steps down?"

"My passion is numbers. But numbers are only a small part of the company." Xavier smiled. "Tyler's passion extends to every-thing: numbers, distribution, software, hardware, technical support."

"Saint Ty." Lauren gave Tyler a cool smile. "Heavy is the head that wears the crown."

"Ty was born to run the company." Donovan met Tyler's gaze. "And he'd be good at it."

The pride in the other men's voices humbled him. Tyler braced his hand on his desk.

"Make the call, Ty." Xavier's words were quiet but firm.

"I will." He waited until the trio left his office.

Tyler resumed his seat, then loaded The Beharie Agency's website. Iris's contact number was on the home page. He tapped it into his phone.

She was his last resort. Would their partnership help him achieve his goal? Or by this time next year, would an outsider be sitting in his father's office?

There was only one way to find out.

CHAPTER 3

Iris turned her cell phone back on as she left her client meeting Thursday afternoon. The voicemail message icon popped onto her display screen. She played the recording as she strode across the parking lot toward her car.

"Iris, this is Ty Anderson of Anderson Adventures."

The unexpected sound of his warm baritone made her knees tremble. Iris paused to steady herself before continuing to her Camry.

"Could you meet with me this afternoon?" He left his phone number and asked her to call him back. His message was time stamped at twelve-eighteen.

Was it possible he'd decided to work with her? Or perhaps he wanted to return her business card. Iris's hands shook as she unlocked her door. She tossed her briefcase onto her backseat. After their last meeting more than a week ago, she'd been pretty confident it would be years — if ever — before Anderson Adventures showed any further interest in her agency. Now, perhaps she was getting that opportunity she'd been hoping for.

She slammed her car door shut, then glanced at her silver Omni wristwatch. Two o'clock in the afternoon. She'd already kept him waiting almost two hours.

Iris got behind the wheel of her Camry and turned the ignition. She took a deep breath, then put on her hands-free device before calling Tyler. Her hands continued to shake.

His line rang three times before Sherry picked up. "Anderson Adventures. Tyler Anderson's office. May I help you?"

"Sherry, it's Iris Beharie. How are you?"

"I'm fine, and you?" There was a smile in the other woman's voice.

"Living the dream, Sherry. Living the dream." Iris pressed the button for her heater. Was it the temperature or her nerves making her hands shake? "I'm returning Ty's call. Is he available?"

"Let me check."

While she waited, Iris navigated out of the parking lot and headed toward her town-home about fifteen minutes away.

"Iris?" Sherry returned to the phone. "Ty's back in his office. Let me put you through."

"Thanks, Sherry. Enjoy the rest of your afternoon."

Iris braced herself for her conversation with Anderson Adventures' vice president of product development.

"Thank you for calling me back." Tyler's voice caused a tremor of pleasure to roll down her spine, in contrast to the tension tightening her shoulders.

She took a settling breath. "Of course. What can I do for you?"

"I'd actually wanted to meet with you in person but your website doesn't have your business address."

Iris stopped at a red light. "I work out of my home."

The screeching silence coming over the phone line screamed, *Wrong answer!* She wouldn't apologize for her cost-cutting measures. Once her business was on more solid ground she'd rent space in a cozy nearby office complex. Until then, she promoted her lack of an office as providing her clients with the convenience of her coming to them.

"You meet with clients in your home?" Tyler sounded as though her one-woman show had gone down even farther in his estimation.

"No, I meet with them in their offices, just as I met with you last week at Anderson Adventures." Iris struggled to focus on Tyler's words. His voice did wicked things to her insides.

The traffic light turned green. Iris pulled into the intersection and continued her drive home.

"I see."

Iris frowned. "Did you ask me to call just so we could chat about office rentals? Is Anderson Adventures looking to expand?"

"Not at this time." There was a tapping in the background as though Tyler was drumming his fingers on the glass surface of his desk. "Actually, Iris, I was calling to give you the contract for our product launch. How soon can you start?"

Did he just offer me the project he didn't think I had a snowball's chance in hell of contractually completing?

"I'm sorry, what did you say?"

"I said we want The Beharie Agency to handle the product launch for 'Osiris's Journey.' "

"What made you change your mind?" Iris pulled into a nearby parking lot. This discussion required her full attention.

Tyler hesitated as though he hadn't anticipated her question. Had he thought she'd jump for joy, then sign the contract before he could change his mind? Anderson Adventures wasn't the only one with a lot to lose.

"Your proposal was very strong and you spoke enthusiastically about the project."

Iris parked in the first open space she found. "We discussed my proposal more than a week ago. At that time, you were adamant that, although my plan was strong, my solo practice didn't inspire your confidence. What's changed?"

She turned off her engine and stared through the windshield. She imagined Tyler, sitting at his desk, surrounded by his computer, minifridge and radio. What had happened to bring the gaming executive back to her?

"I've changed my mind."

The lightbulb came on in Iris's brain. "The larger company didn't work out, did they? What happened? Did they charge too much money? They couldn't commit to your launch schedule?"

"That's not relevant. The fact of the matter is —"

"Come clean, Ty. If we're going to be working together, we can't have secrets between us."

Another pause. "I'm not used to vendors being so . . ."

"Assertive?"

"I was going to say bold."

Iris smiled. Did he think she'd be insulted? "You've never worked with me."

Tyler gave her a noncommittal "hmm." "The other company didn't respond to my request for a proposal."

Iris snapped her fingers. "Poor customer service. You know, I almost said that. Actually, I should have said that before guessing they'd asked for too much money. After all, Anderson Adventures is a multimillion-dollar company. You could probably afford to contract with two large consulting businesses."

She'd love to know what company had been stupid enough to ignore a proposal request from Anderson Adventures.

Tyler sighed. "Iris? Do you want the contract?"

"I'm not comfortable working for a client who doubts my abilities." She watched a squirrel race up the evergreen tree planted in front of her car. It scurried away, disappearing into the branches. "You won't trust my opinions and you'll second-guess my actions."

Her last boss had made her justify every thought she had, every move she made — then had taken credit for her successes. She couldn't work like that — no matter how badly she wanted this account.

"You're launching an Anderson Adventures product. I have to approve your marketing strategy. I'm hiring your company but you're representing mine." Tyler's tone was persuasive. It was as though, now that he'd set his mind to hiring her, he wasn't going to take no for an answer.

"You're hiring my expertise. If I tell you something will or won't work, I need you to respect that."

"As long as you're willing to discuss your reasoning."

Iris hesitated a moment more. The bottom line was she wanted this account. She still had her reservations because of his low expectation of her abilities. But she wanted the opportunity to prove to Tyler Anderson that what he'd considered second best had been the right choice all along.

"Fair enough. I'll accept your offer. Thank you."

"Good." Tyler seemed relieved. "How soon can you start?"

Iris arched a brow at his anxious tone. "I take it you haven't postponed your product launch?"

"No, we haven't."

Of course not. "Then I'll see you at eight o'clock tomorrow morning."

"Thank you, Iris."

Had she actually gotten a smile out of the product developer? "Enjoy your afternoon, Ty."

Iris disconnected the call, then restarted her car. Something told her she'd have an uphill battle with Anderson Adventures' vice president of product development. Tyler didn't appear to impress easily. But that's what she'd have to do to ensure the success of this account and future client recommendations.

This was the opportunity she'd been working toward. She had until eight o'clock tomorrow morning to come up with a detailed plan for the product launch — and another to avoid being distracted by Tyler Anderson.

"Why do we need an internal launch?" Tyler sounded as if he needed more coffee.

Iris's gaze moved from his irritated ebony eyes to the large silver-and-black mug beside her new client's right hand. *Should I suggest he get a refill? No, that would probably offend him.*

She sat back on the cushioned chair at his conversation table and refocused on their Friday-morning meeting. "I'm sure details of 'Osiris's Journey' have been kept from most — if not all — of your employees to prevent leaks."

"That's right. We don't want the public — or our competitors — to hear about it in advance."

"Most successful corporate campaigns grow from the inside out. Before you launch your latest game nationally, you should give your employees a sneak peek. It's a morale booster."

"Foster sends a companywide email before each release." Tyler noted something on his electronic tablet. "But since I'm handling this launch, he'll probably want the message to come from me. I'll check with him."

That was more than a lot of companies did but still not enough. "Your employees should know about more than just the game. Tell them how you're going to launch it — key dates, media outlets, talking points. They'll share that information with family, friends, members of their community organizations. It's free word-of-mouth advertising."

"We can put that in the email." Tyler continued typing.

"With all due respect, Ty, an email's not enough." Iris watched his long, elegant fingers move across the tablet's keyboard. The sight was distracting. She raised her eyes. "The majority of company emails aren't read. If you want employees to receive your message, your best bet is talking with them face-to-face."

They locked gazes. This was their first disagreement — and the first item on her agenda. If she had to debate each of the four topics with him, it was going to be a long meeting. She glanced at her coffee mug. *I wonder if I should get a refill?*

Tyler finally nodded. "Those are good points."

"Thank you." Iris wanted to pump her fist in victory. She settled for handing him another sheet of paper from her manila project folder. "This is a draft schedule of your internal launch, including tasks. I've also emailed it to you. We can review it once we're done with the other agenda items."

"This is a lot of detail. When did you put this together?"

The admiration in Tyler's tone made Iris pause. "Last night."

"Thank you." Those two words expressed more than gratitude. She heard respect, appreciation and relief.

"You're welcome."

Thankfully, they moved through the rest of the agenda at a much faster pace. At least until they came to the media interviews.

"Why do I have to do so many of them?" Surly best described Tyler's tone.

"I'm going to pitch your release to these outlets — print, as well as broadcast and podcasts. That doesn't mean all of these venues will agree to an interview."

"Our previous marketing consultant just sent out press releases. We've never done pitches before."

"That's not a good enough reason not to do them now." How much had their previous consultant charged to attach a release to an email and hit Send? Iris cringed just thinking about it.

"Don't you think this is going overboard?" Tyler gestured toward her media proposal.

"Not at all." Iris was firm. "Your three most recent product releases have been on the list of the top-ten most popular computer games for almost a year. Candidly, I think every media outlet all over the country will jump at the chance to interview you. We should do as many of them as we can."

"I can't be away from the office for weeks at a time." Tyler looked harassed. "We're working on other games."

"We'll only do what your schedule will allow. Some of these can be done over the phone." Iris checked that item off of their agenda. "You showed me some of the features of 'Osiris's Journey.' I'm not familiar with computer games but I was impressed by yours."

"Thank you."

"But it's not what I expected." Iris's eyebrows knitted. "Why did you create the game?"

Tyler seemed deep in thought as he sipped his coffee. "We designed 'Osiris's Journey' to introduce teens and preteens to Egyptian mythology."

"Osiris is considered the king of the afterlife."

Tyler nodded. "For example, he's credited with the harvest and renewal of crops, the flooding of the Nile, the rising and setting of the sun. The game is a series of battles between Osiris and his brother, Seth, who murdered him and cut his body into fourteen pieces. Seth is the god of storms and the desert."

"It looks like an exciting game. I'm glad that you included Osiris's wife, Isis, as well."

"Isis is critical to Osiris's story." Tyler's deep voice quickened with enthusiasm.

"After Seth cut Osiris's body into fourteen pieces, Isis searched their kingdom until she found each one. Then she used her magic to put him back together and bring him back to life."

"I'm familiar with their mythology. It's such a bittersweet love story. She was really devoted to him." What would it be like to have someone love her that much? Sometimes she wondered whether she'd ever find love, true love.

Iris set the thought aside and moved on to the next agenda item, social media. "I couldn't find Anderson Adventures on Facebook or Twitter. Do you have those accounts?"

"No." Tyler looked as though she'd asked if he'd ever traveled off planet.

Iris's eyebrows knitted in confusion. "You sell computer games. Your audience is on the internet. Anderson Adventures needs to get on the social media bandwagon — Facebook, Twitter, Pinterest, Instagram —"

"Slow down." Tyler held up a hand. "We don't have the staff to maintain those sites."

"I can get us started for now." Iris watched him lower his hand. "We'll discuss your hiring college interns to maintain the sites once I'm gone."

"All right." But he didn't sound happy

about it.

"You're a computer gaming company." Iris swallowed back her growing agitation. "It's critically important for you to be active on social media. Your customers are there."

"We've never had a marketing consultant tell us any of this before." Tyler stared down at the meeting agenda as though it was a death warrant. "This partnership is going to change the company in ways I'd never imagined."

"That's a good thing." Iris surrendered to her indignation. "Your previous marketing consultants should have set up your social media platforms. They should have given you a plan on how to run it. What were you paying them for?"

Tyler was silent for several rapid heartbeats. His ebony eyes searched each of her features as though he was looking for something. "You're right. I'm glad you're here, Iris."

A slow blush warmed her cheeks. Iris's unsteady gaze dropped. He was glad she was here for the product launch. She knew that's what he'd meant. Then why did she want him to mean something more?

Tyler's caller identification screen displayed

Kimball & Associates' phone number. So, his former marketing consulting firm had decided to return his messages. It was after five o'clock on Friday afternoon, more than a week after the proposal deadline.

Where had they been this morning, before he'd signed the contract with Iris — and barely survived their first project meeting? Better yet, where had they been a week ago, when he'd called to ask for their proposal? He swallowed a sigh and picked up the phone.

"Tyler Anderson." His voice was tight.

"Ty! It's Pete Kimball. How are you?"

"Fine, Pete. How can I help you?"

Peter must have keyed into Tyler's cool tone. He pumped up the energy and enthusiasm in his voice as though hoping to break through the ice. "Hey, thank you for giving us an opportunity to submit a proposal for your launch. I'm getting ready to send it over to you now."

Tyler rubbed his eyes. "It's March twentieth. The deadline was more than a week ago."

"I know, Ty. We've just been so lousy busy around here lately."

"Is that the reason you didn't return my messages? I left several."

"Yeah, it's just been crazy. I'm really sorry

66

about that."

"I'm sorry, too, Pete." Tyler went back to the summary he was drafting on the latest test results for "Osiris's Journey." They were dismal. And he was running out of time. "There's no point in your submitting a proposal. I've already awarded the contract."

"You have?" Peter sounded stunned.

What had he expected, that Anderson Adventures would sit and wait forever for their proposal?

"Yes and we've signed a contract." Tyler typed in the date and time of the next game test and recommendations for improvements. "As I explained in my request for your proposal, we're on a very tight time frame for the launch. That's one of the reasons I left so many messages for you." *Pity you never responded to any of them.*

"I see."

"Goodbye, Pete."

"Wait! Do you mind if I ask who won the contract?"

Tyler hesitated but didn't see any harm in telling Peter he was working with Iris. "The Beharie Agency."

"*Iris* Beharie?" Peter sounded as though Tyler had contracted with an alien life form.

"Do you know her?"

"Yes, I do." The consultant's tone was

grim. "Listen, Ty. There's something you should know about her."

CHAPTER 4

Standing at her stove Friday evening, Iris wasn't especially curious when her front doorbell chimed a little after six o'clock. It couldn't be anyone she knew. Family and friends pulled in behind her garage and knocked at her back door. She turned off the fire beneath the boiling pot of water — the spaghetti would have to wait — then padded in stocking feet out of her kitchen and across her living room. Iris rose up on her toes to check the peephole — and gasped.

What is Ty Anderson doing at my door?

She grabbed the knot of hair she'd clipped to the top of her head. Horrified, she looked at her oversized sweatshirt and faded red tights with the name of Cleveland's professional basketball team written on the legs.

Oh, my word! I can't let a client see me like this.

The doorbell rang again. Iris's panicked,

gaze leaped up the stairs. But if Tyler couldn't wait one minute for her to answer his summons, there was no way Mr. Impatience would cool his heels while she pulled on a power suit.

Iris channeled her older sister, Rose. *Assume control, project confidence.* She pulled open her front door. "Ty. What a surprise. I believe I mentioned I never conduct client meetings in my home."

"We need to talk." His somber expression alarmed her.

Iris stepped aside, gesturing him in. "What's wrong?"

Tyler crossed her threshold before turning to face her. "Why didn't you tell me you were fired from RGB for unethical behavior?"

A hundred words flashed across Iris's mind. Several of them were quite unprofessional. She kept a grip on her temper by channeling her inner Lily. *Remain calm; get the facts.*

Iris counted to twenty while she closed and locked her front door against the chill of the late-March evening. She faced Tyler, keeping her arms at her sides and her gaze level with his. "What makes you think RGB fired me?"

"My sources in the industry told me."

His sources? The lightbulb clicked on. *Pete Kimball, that nasty, little troll.* Iris drew a deeper breath. How did Lily maintain her serenity?

"Your sources are incorrect." She tilted her head. "Are you interested in the truth?"

"Of course." Tyler crossed his arms over his broad chest.

Iris gave him a once-over. His teak wool overcoat masked his long, lean form. His ebony eyes burned with outrage and . . . betrayal? Did he think she'd broken his trust? She had too much personal integrity to do something like that. But of course Tyler wouldn't know that because he didn't know her.

Iris led him the few steps into her living room and gestured toward her chunky, emerald sofa. "Have a seat." The invitation went against her grain. She'd never intended to entertain clients in her home. But by showing up on her doorstep and questioning her character, he'd left her no choice.

Tyler hesitated a second or two before shrugging off his overcoat and following her instructions. Iris didn't take his coat. He wouldn't be staying that long.

"What happened at RGB?" Tyler set his coat on the cushion beside him.

Iris settled onto her matching love seat.

"RGB was my second job out of college. I'd worked there for more than five years as a public relations coordinator. Meanwhile, other people with less experience and ability than me were advanced ahead of me because they either had the look the executives wanted or their father knew someone in management."

"The old boys' club." Tyler's tone was dry.

"Exactly." Iris crossed her legs and folded her arms. Her stomach still churned at the injustice. She'd never forget it. "I'm not proud of the fact that I played their game for so long. I thought my hard work and dedication would be rewarded. Instead, I behaved like the definition of insanity."

"You were literally doing the same thing over and over again, and expecting a different result." Tyler's eyes no longer burned with the fires of retribution. They'd softened with an empathy Iris was even less comfortable with.

"That's right." She lifted her chin, defiant. "I was passed over for a fourth time for an account executive position. Management promoted the son of one of the vice president's friends. My consolation prize was being assigned to his team provided I did his work."

Tyler frowned. "If they wanted *you* to do

his work, why did they give *him* the job?"

"His father wanted him to have the title and pay." Iris swung her right calf in short, stiff movements. "And to take the credit."

"Unbelievable. What did you do?"

"That's probably where the claims of unethical behavior come in." Iris didn't hesitate. "I told them in anatomically correct terms what they could do with their offer and how they could do it. But I didn't give them the chance to fire me. I quit. I can show you the email if you doubt me."

Tyler's eyebrows leapt up his high forehead. "You responded in an email?"

"Maybe *that's* how Pete Kimball got the idea that my behavior was unethical."

"Who mentioned Pete Kimball?" Tyler's enigmatic expression didn't fool Iris.

"It's simple deduction, Sherlock." Iris stopped swinging her leg. "Pete Kimball wants your account. And he knows I have it."

The marketing consultant was on to him. Tyler looked away. He wouldn't — couldn't — lie to her. And he was glad she'd stopped swinging her leg. He'd been distracted by those shapely limbs in the faded, red leggings. About half of his bluster had been his attempt to mask his reaction to them.

73

His fingers twitched, itching to remove the clip binding her sable tresses. But the style emphasized her elegant, warm-honey features: high cheekbones, long nose, that Cupid's bow mouth. He could blissfully drown in her wide, coffee eyes.

Tyler pulled his gaze from Iris's face and let it roam over her living room. The decor reflected the woman: modern, well put together, bold; from the large emerald sofa and matching love seat, to the sterling-silver-and-onyx entertainment center and matching coffee table. Three of the walls were painted pure white. The wall behind the entertainment center was deep red. The lamp on the silver-and-onyx corner table was carved from stone. The beige wall-to-wall carpet must have come with the town-home.

"I'm sorry I accused you instead of asking for an explanation." Tyler's attention dropped to the magazine spread open on her coffee table. It was the latest issue of a computer gaming publication.

"Corporate espionage is a hot-button issue in the gaming industry." Iris shrugged. "Being told you've hired an ethically challenged consultant probably didn't sit well with you."

"I appreciate your understanding."

"Now that we've gotten that straightened out, I'm going to settle in for the evening." She stood, unfolding her arms. "I've got a lot of work to do to prepare for your executive team meeting Monday morning."

I'm being dismissed. Tyler suppressed a smile as he rose from Iris's sofa. "Of course. I'm sorry to barge in on you at home."

"I'm glad we talked it through." Iris led him to her door. "Once you get to know me, you'll realize you can trust me. I understand and respect your need for confidentiality."

Tyler jerked his attention from her hips. He shouldn't be checking out his consultant. "Thank you."

Iris opened her front door, pulling it wider as she stepped back. "Enjoy the rest of your weekend."

Tyler stepped over the threshold, then looked back at her. "Should we get together to discuss the agenda for Monday's meeting?"

Her winged eyebrows knitted. "We already discussed most of it when we met this morning."

"All right. Good." He hadn't felt this awkward around a female since puberty. "One thing we didn't discuss, though, was where you'll be working."

She frowned. "I usually work out of my office."

"I think it would better for you to work out of ours." *Where had that come from?*

"Why?" Iris looked as startled as Tyler felt.

"You pointed out yourself that we're on a tight schedule, which is even tighter since you insist on an internal launch."

"The internal launch is the right thing to do for your employees."

"I've conceded that." Tyler propped his shoulder against the doorjamb and looked into her eyes. "But it will be more efficient for us to work together if you're near me."

"I'm working on projects for other clients, as well."

"Are any of those projects as big as Anderson Adventures' launches?"

"Of course not."

"Then you can fit them in around our launches while you're working in our office."

Their eyes locked in a contest of wills. Tyler sensed Iris's struggle to construct counterarguments. He'd never worked with a consultant like Iris. She obviously didn't subscribe to the belief that the customer was always right. But whereas she'd won the battle of the internal launch, Tyler was determined to win this contest. It might be his only victory during the entire project.

Her slender shoulders rose and fell beneath her oversize NBA sweatshirt. "All right. I'll work out of your office."

"Thank you." Tyler straightened from her door. "I'll see you Monday, then."

"I guess you will."

Tyler couldn't conquer this smile. She'd sounded so annoyed. "We'll get you set up with an office and a security key card." He turned and strode to his car without waiting for her response.

If absence made the heart grow fonder, maybe seeing Iris every day would lessen his growing attraction to the marketing consultant. Somehow, he doubted it.

The Anderson Adventures executive team looked bright and alert, as though they'd been up for hours. It was only eight o'clock. Iris wasn't used to interacting with such energetic executives so early, especially on a Monday morning. What was their secret? Was it the coffee?

"I'll make the introductions." Tyler sat beside Iris on one side of the large sterling silver–framed Plexiglas conference table. He gestured toward the distinguished older gentleman at the head of the table. "Foster Anderson is our CEO. He founded this company with his brother, Gray."

Foster inclined his head. "Good to meet you."

"You, as well." Iris recognized Tyler's father from photos she'd found on the internet. Those images hadn't done him justice.

In person, Foster Anderson was an attractive, charismatic figure. Father and son bore a close resemblance: perfect sienna skin; square, chiseled features; long, broad nose; full, sensual lips. In fact, all of the Anderson Adventures men were easy on the eyes. They looked more like classic Hollywood heartthrobs than stereotypical computer nerds.

Focus, Iris.

Tyler gestured toward the opposite end of the table where the only other woman in the room sat. "My aunt, Kayla Cooper Anderson, is a member of our executive team."

Kayla's large onyx eyes twinkled. "Thank you for coming, Iris."

"Thank you for the opportunity." Iris admired the timeless woman's grace and style. She wore an ice-blue skirt suit. Her glossy, still-dark hair was swept up and back in a chignon, displaying understated but expensive pearl earrings that matched her necklace.

Tyler continued the introductions. "Xavier

Anderson is our vice president of finance."

From her research, Iris knew Kayla was Gray Anderson's widow and Xavier was their only child.

"Good morning." Xavier had his mother's eyes, minus their warmth. Instead they were onyx laser beams, trying to bore their way into her mind.

"How do you do, Mr. Anderson?" Iris returned the finance officer's steady gaze.

"We're all on a first-name basis." The final member of the team interrupted the introductions.

Tyler grinned, waving a hand across the table. "And, of course, Donovan 'Van' Carroll, our vice president of sales."

Iris inclined her head toward the sales executive. "Good morning, Van."

"Hi." With that simple greeting and a killer smile, Donovan settled back onto his chair. His broad shoulders were relaxed beneath his long-sleeved garnet-colored shirt. His demeanor gave the impression he was spending the evening with friends at a jazz club rather than sitting through an early-morning business meeting.

All eyes were on Iris. She took a breath and wished for a little of Donovan's calm. Instead her efforts to ease the butterflies battling in her stomach were futile. There was a lot riding on this account: her self-image, her sisters' respect, her livelihood.

Don't think about those things right now . . .

She straightened in her chair and returned the gazes of the other people around the table. "I want your thoughts regarding Anderson Adventures' next product launch. As I explained to Ty, I strongly believe we should first host an internal launch to support your external campaign."

"Why?" Xavier's question wasn't unexpected. Like most finance officers, his first concern was the budget.

Iris met Xavier's gaze. "Every Anderson Adventures employee is an unofficial member of your sales team."

"We prefer the term associates." Donovan sat forward. "But you're right."

"Associates. Excuse me." Iris made a note of the term, then resumed her explanation. "Imagine that, shortly after 'Osiris's Journey' is introduced to the media, Sherry's neighbor asks her about it. Without the internal launch, Sherry couldn't tell her neighbor anything he didn't already know about the game. With the internal launch, Sherry would find out about the game directly from you and could ask her own questions. She'd then have insight her neighbor wouldn't have read in the media.

As a result, he'd be even more enthusiastic about the game."

Donovan added to her narrative. "And, if her experience with the internal launch was positive, her neighbor would pick up on her excitement."

"Exactly." Iris smiled at Donovan. With his sales background, he understood her point. "Your associates also could help create a buzz about 'Osiris's Journey' on their social media sites."

Foster gave her a considering look. "We've never had an internal launch before, although Van has suggested associate meetings."

"But I was outvoted." Donovan shrugged good-naturedly. "Instead, we sent a company-wide email."

Iris winced. "That strategy is well-intentioned. But it lacks the personal touch. And not every associate reads the email."

"Well, Iris, no one has ever explained the impact to us so clearly. Thank you," Kayla added.

Why hadn't their other marketing consultant reviewed this simple concept with them?

This wasn't the first time Anderson Adventures had contracted with a marketing firm. Although obviously profitable, like most companies these days, it operated with a lean staff. From her research, Iris knew the gaming company had a strong sales force, and a sizeable research and development team. But support departments such as human resources, accounting and marketing were slim. Most of the functions those departments performed were outsourced, which kept consulting firms such as hers in business.

Xavier crossed his forearms, bunching impressive biceps beneath the long sleeves of his bronze shirt. He shot a look toward Tyler and Foster before settling again on her. "It appears the marketing firms we've contracted with in the past didn't give us our money's worth."

Kayla cocked her head. "Didn't Loretta work for one of those firms?"

Xavier seemed surprised. "Her name's Lauren and she doesn't work for a marketing firm."

Tyler and Donovan exchanged a look. It was similar to the silent communication Iris shared with Rose when Lily was on the edge, or with Lily when Rose was ready to blow a gasket.

Kayla continued. "Well, going forward, we now understand the value of an internal launch. Thank you, Iris."

Donovan raised a hand. "I'd like to point out that, if anyone had listened to me, you'd have understood its importance years ago."

"A prophet is never appreciated in his own time." Tyler's voice was somber though his ebony eyes twinkled with mischief.

So, the vice president of product development does have a sense of humor.

The words and reactions directed toward Donovan Carroll made it clear that he was part of the family despite his different surname. In fact, this planning session felt more like a family discussion than a corporate meeting.

Foster returned to the agenda. "What's our next step?"

Iris shifted her smile from Tyler's and Donovan's antics to Foster. "We need to determine the type of internal launch. Simple or elaborate? Serious or festive? Do you envision an associate meeting or an event?"

"I'm sure I can guess what type of launch you'd prefer." Xavier's tone was dry.

Iris's cheeks warmed. " 'Osiris's Journey' is an exciting product. I don't think a simple associate meeting would do it justice."

"Iris is right." Kayla addressed Xavier. " 'Osiris's Journey' is worth an event rather than a boring old meeting. If Lisa made the suggestion, you know you'd agree."

Xavier sighed. "Her name's Lauren, Mom. And associate meetings don't have to be boring."

"But they are." Kayla's nod added emphasis. "Don't you agree, Iris?"

"I agree with Iris and Kayla." Donovan's interruption saved Iris from responding.

"How elaborate are you thinking?" Xavier propped his forearms on the glass table.

"You're just thinking of the price." Kayla crossed her arms.

Xavier gave his mother a look. "Someone has to."

Kayla sighed. "You wouldn't be so focused on the cost if this was Lori's idea."

"Lauren," Xavier corrected. "And yes, I would."

Why couldn't Kayla remember Xavier's girlfriend's name? The older woman didn't have any trouble remembering Iris's name and they'd just met.

"Xavier has a point, Aunt Kayla." Tyler spoke up. "If the goal is to give associates information to help sell the product, why does the meeting have to be elaborate?"

"This isn't just about information. It's about people, *our* people." Foster's quiet response carried a wealth of meaning and messages. "We want to show our associates that we care about them. They're an important and strategic part of this launch."

"Understood." Tyler's tone was respectful but Iris heard the tension in his voice.

"So, we're going with a bigger launch." Xavier held Iris's gaze. "Don't break the budget."

Iris smiled to reassure him. This wasn't her first rodeo. "I can produce a dynamic launch on a budget."

"That's why we hired you, Iris." Kayla inclined her head.

"Let's get started." Tyler pushed away from the table, signaling the meeting was over.

Iris stood, pausing to wish the other members of the meeting a good day. Donovan seemed satisfied by the meeting's outcome. Xavier appeared concerned. Kayla looked pleased.

But it was the strain on Foster's expression that stayed with Iris. What had put that look on his face?

Iris was getting the feeling that there was more at stake with this launch than just the success of "Osiris's Journey."

CHAPTER 5

Tension twisted the muscles in Tyler's neck and shoulders as he escorted Iris away from the executive conference room and down the aisle that led to Sherry.

Why was his father second-guessing him?

Why had Iris smiled at Donovan?

Why do I care?

"That was one of the most efficient executive meetings I've ever attended." Iris seemed impressed. "And one of the shortest."

"We don't have time for unproductive meetings." Tyler stopped beside the administrative assistant's desk. "Hi, Sherry. Do you have Iris's key card?"

"I sure do." Sherry pulled a small rectangular cream card from a side desk drawer. The Anderson Adventures logo was set in large black type in the center of the card's hard plastic surface. She offered it to Iris, along with a black-and-silver lanyard.

"It's good to see you again, Iris."

"You, too, Sherry." Iris accepted the items.

After two meetings, Iris and Sherry seemed like friends. In contrast, after more than two months, Lauren didn't know Sherry's name. But then, Kayla couldn't remember Lauren's name, either. That wasn't like his aunt.

Tyler set aside his concern for now. "Keep your key card with you at all times. Most doors on this floor — including this entrance — and our research floor downstairs are kept locked."

Sherry lifted her key card, which she wore suspended from the lanyard around her neck. "No one wants to be locked out of the office after a bathroom break."

"See you later, Sherry." Tyler started back down the hallway. "You may have noticed most of us prop our office doors open." He glanced at Iris. Was she still thinking of Donovan? Was she attracted to his friend? "The doors lock automatically when they're shut. Always lock your computer and close your door when you leave your office."

"That's going to take some getting used to." Iris's shoulder-length, sable hair shone beneath the office suite's fluorescent lights. "Why do I have to lock my computer if the office door automatically locks?"

"It's an added precaution."

"Is this security meant to prevent corporate espionage?" Iris's eyes searched his. "I've read there's a lot of spying in the computer gaming industry."

"We trust our employees. The security measures give us an added comfort level." Tyler passed his office and stopped in front of a small conference room, which would serve as Iris's office for the duration of the project. "Let's see if your key card works." His pulse kicked up with the knowledge she would be steps from him for the next four months. *Keep it professional, Ty. She's your consultant. That's all.*

Iris swiped the card through the lock on the glass door. A green light blinked and she let herself into the conference room.

The space was bright and spare: six gray cushioned chairs surrounded a rectangular glass-and-sterling-silver table. A gray metal filing cabinet stood in one corner. A small blond wood table was tucked into another. Three glass-framed photographs lined the beige wall behind the table. One was of the current building, which Anderson Adventures had moved into ten years before. The middle picture was a black-and-white image of the first space the business had rented. The third picture, also black-

and-white, showed a very small dining room.

Iris studied the last photograph. "Is this where your father and uncle started Anderson Adventures?"

"Yes. It's the dining room of the apartment they shared when they first graduated from college."

"Your family's come a long way." Iris stepped back and scanned the supplies and equipment arranged at the head of the table.

"Ted from IT will come up later to connect you to the printer." Tyler pointed toward her telephone. "Your extension, fax number and other codes are on the paper beside your computer."

"Great." She lowered herself onto her chair. "I'll get started on the plans for the internal launch."

"There's one other thing." Tyler hesitated. Something had to be said, though. Right?

Iris looked up at him. "What is it?"

His mind shouted that he was making a mistake. *Don't say anything. Leave it alone. Just turn and walk away.* But he couldn't tear from his mind the image of Donovan smiling at her — and of her smiling back.

His mouth kept moving. "As our contracted vendor, you have to adhere to the same office policies as our employees."

"That won't be a problem."

"That means no office romances." He tried but he couldn't stop talking.

"All right." Iris's brow creased. Tyler sensed her confusion.

"That includes Van."

She blinked. "Excuse me?"

"During the meeting, you smiled at him."

"And you interpreted my smile as flirtation?"

When she said it like that, it sounded really stupid. This time, Tyler was able to keep his mouth shut.

"I realize you don't know me, but I'm asking you to step out on faith and trust me." Iris's eyes cooled. Her voice was even colder.

"I want to be clear that you're here for the product launch — and that's all." He was making things worse.

"We're crystal clear," Iris's voice dropped another ten degrees.

"Good." Tyler fought the urge to fidget under her glare. "If you need anything, let me know."

"How about a little trust?"

Tyler hesitated. He didn't want Iris to be angry. For one thing, they needed to work together. But he didn't want her to flirt with Donovan, either. She wouldn't be the first woman to fall for the sales executive's good looks and natural charm. He just didn't want her to be the next.

"I'm sure the trust will come." Tyler turned to leave. Part of him believed he could trust her. Then what was holding him back? The part that worried that, with Iris, he had more at stake than the product launch.

"How's your first day with your newest client going?" Cathy took a huge bite of her frosted fudge-walnut brownie while her soup and sandwich lay untouched.

"This morning, Tyler Anderson accused me of using his company as a matchmaking service." Iris stirred sweetener into her hazelnut coffee.

"What?" Cathy's interjection triggered an unfortunate coughing fit.

While her friend caught her breath, Iris surveyed their surroundings. The little café where they were meeting for lunch was within walking distance of Anderson Adventures' offices in Columbus's Short North district. Several of the gaming company's employees were at nearby tables. They'd greeted her with curious smiles and nods of recognition.

Iris sipped her coffee. She and Cathy were using their lunch break to review the progress of several joint projects. Normally, they'd meet at one of their home offices. However, since Iris had allowed Tyler to talk her into using an office at Anderson Adventures — *how did he convince me to do that?* — Cathy had agreed to meet here.

"Why would he say that?" Her friend had regained enough breath for a follow-up question to Iris's matchmaking comment.

"Because I smiled at one of the other vice presidents." Iris gritted her teeth over the absurdity of Tyler's accusation and his supposed basis for it.

Cathy gaped. "Is he nuts?"

Why did the question make Iris a little defensive for the high-powered computer geek? She shrugged off the feeling with a restless movement of her shoulders. "I think he's under a great deal of pressure."

"I don't care how stressed out he is." Cathy scowled. "He shouldn't have said that to you."

Iris didn't disagree. "I have a feeling a lot is riding on this game launch. And we've gotten a late start."

"Whose fault is that?"

Iris smiled at her friend's unwavering support. Sometimes the little designer was like an overprotective pit bull. "This is also the first time he's led a product launch."

"Stop defending him." Her friend waved both arms in an impatient gesture. "He was way out of line."

Cathy was right. Tyler had crossed the line. *Then why am I making excuses for him?*

Iris dropped her gaze to her sandwich. But instead of turkey and provolone on rye, she saw Tyler's chiseled sienna features, penetrating ebony eyes, leanly muscled frame and tight, tempting glutes. She put a lid on her rising attraction. Being tall, dark and handsome didn't give him a pass.

"You're right." Iris picked up her sandwich. "There's no excuse for his accusation. It was insulting and unprofessional. I'm just trying to understand his perspective."

"Don't." Cathy's tone was firm. "Instead of getting in touch with Tyler Anderson's feelings, you need to work on strategies to protect yourself."

"From what?"

"His warped sense of reality." Cathy snorted. "Make sure you continue to act in a professional manner. You have to remain above reproach. And document everything."

Iris swallowed a bite of her sandwich. Now that her appetite had disappeared, the turkey and provolone tasted like sawdust. "I know all of this, Cathy."

"Obviously, you need to be reminded. Remember, he didn't want you."

Iris caught her breath. "No, he didn't." The words hurt more than they should. Why? Tyler Anderson was just a client.

After vanquishing her brownie, Cathy dug into her chicken-noodle soup as though she hadn't eaten in days. The gray scarf around the neckline of her black blouse hung close to the bowl. "No doubt he's looking for you to slip up and show some kind of weakness to prove he'd been right in the first place and shouldn't have hired you."

"But he did hire me."

"He never should have hesitated in the first place." Cathy adjusted the length of her scarf with jerky motions, pulling it away from her soup bowl. "But he only came to his senses after Kimball & Associates ignored his request for a bid. That doesn't mean he has faith in you. He may be digging for evidence that his first instincts were right."

Iris shook her head. "Any mistakes could put his product launch and his company in jeopardy. Why would he want that?"

"You know these corporate types." Cathy gave her a superior look. "They're not rational."

"They say the same thing about designers." Iris could understand why. She considered her friend, seated on the other side of the small square table.

"You need to protect yourself." Cathy apparently chose to ignore Iris's comment. "Play it cool. No personal conversations — you're all about business."

"You know that's not me. I'm naturally outgoing. I can't be something I'm not." She wished she could. Something told her she would need to keep her guard up around Tyler. Iris stared morosely at her sandwich.

"You have to try. You're too trusting. That's one of the reasons RGB was able to take advantage of you for so long."

"Anderson Adventures isn't RGB."

Cathy lowered her half-eaten sandwich. "What does he look like?"

"What does who look like?" Iris squirmed under her friend's narrow-eyed stare.

"You know who I'm talking about. Tyler Anderson. What does he look like?"

"You know. Tall. Fit." Iris shrugged. Her gaze darted around the little café, landing anywhere but on her friend.

"Handsome?"

"Very."

"That explains why you keep defending him." Cathy's sigh seemed exaggerated. "Don't allow your client's good looks to

95

make you lose sight of your goal. You've got one foot in the door. You need to get the rest of your body through it, too. I'm not just saying this because I'm working on the designs for your project."

"I know that."

Cathy leaned into the table. Her tone became more urgent. "Once you pull off their product launch, Anderson Adventures will realize you're the best marketing consultant they've ever had. They'll keep coming back to you."

"And hopefully other companies will want to work with me, too." Iris sent up a prayer.

"They will." Cathy's earnest expression softened with a smile. "Pretty soon, people will be asking, 'Kimball & Associates, who?'"

"Tempting." Iris's chuckle went a long way toward easing her tension. "But I don't wish any ill will on Pete Kimball."

"That makes one of us," her friend said dryly. "But, Iris, this plan won't succeed if you allow yourself to be distracted by a pretty face."

Or a set of broad shoulders. "Don't worry, Cathy. I'm not about to ruin this opportunity. I can stay focused on the job."

Her mind was willing. Hopefully, her body wouldn't be weak.

■ ■ ■ ■

Tyler stood outside Donovan's office Monday afternoon. He was still stinging from his last encounter with Iris. His request that she maintain a strictly professional relationship with the vice president of sales couldn't have gone worse. Maybe he'd misinterpreted that look between them. He didn't think so. But just in case, he should also have a talk with Donovan. It was only fair. But what was his concern? That their beautiful marketing consultant was attracted to his best friend? The possibility only bothered him because it was unprofessional; not because he had a personal agenda.

Tyler knocked on Donovan's open door, shaking off the uneasy feeling that he was making another mistake. "Van, do you have a minute?"

"Sure." Donovan spun his chair from his computer and faced him. "What's up?"

Tyler's gaze shifted from his friend to the Excel file on the computer screen behind the sales executive. His shoulders slumped in resignation. "You've forgotten to lock your computer. Again."

"But I'm sitting right here."

"I've told you that doesn't matter. You

97

should develop the habit of locking your computer when you're not using it. It's a security precaution." His IT and product-development staffs were the only ones who appreciated the importance of computer security. Everyone else, including his father, needed constant reminders.

"Do you think a competitor will teleport into my office and steal my computer while we're talking?"

"Get into the habit of locking it so —"

"So it will be second nature whenever I step away."

"You do listen to me."

"Do I have a choice?" Donovan tapped a couple of computer keys before turning back to Tyler. "We have this conversation every time you come to my office."

"We wouldn't have it at all if you'd lock your computer."

"Did you come all the way down the hall just to nag me? If so, you've accomplished your mission." Donovan waved. His hazel eyes twinkled. "Have a nice day."

There's my opening. Where do I begin?

Tyler crossed into Donovan's cluttered office. How could his friend keep anything straight? File folders layered his desk. Industry periodicals grew from his conversation table. Advertising schedules littered his bulletin board. Even from across the room, Tyler could tell several of the advertisements had been completed. Why hadn't Donovan archived the schedules? The sales executive swore he had a system. What could it possibly be?

"I didn't come to lecture you about computer security. That was just a lucky coincidence." Tyler took a seat in front of Donovan's desk. His friend had discarded his jacket and rolled the sleeves of his brown jersey to his elbows. "What did you think of the meeting this morning?"

"It went well." Donovan folded his hands on his desk. "I'm excited that we're finally going to have an internal launch. I know you and Xavier have concerns. But trust me, an internal launch will boost our external campaign, especially in this age of social media. What did you think?"

Proceed with caution. "You and Iris appeared to be on the same page."

"That's not surprising." A smile eased into Donovan's eyes. "Sales and marketing philosophies are similar."

"It seemed to be more than professional interest."

Donovan gave Tyler a considering look. In the silence, Tyler heard the murmur of a song coming from the CD player beside the computer.

"I hadn't realized you were so perceptive, Ty." Donovan's voice was grave. "You're right. I felt a strong and instant attraction for Iris the minute she walked into the conference room. She's a very beautiful woman. She's smart, friendly, sexy as —"

"Hold on." Tyler raised one hand and interrupted Donovan's words. "She's also our consultant."

"I know."

"You can't have a personal relationship with our business consultant."

"Why not?"

Tyler gave the other man an incredulous look. "Your feelings for her could influence your decisions."

"*I'm* not the one working with her. *You* are." Donovan chuckled, leaning back on his chair.

It wasn't the first time Tyler hadn't gotten his friend's sense of humor. In fact, Donovan's hilarity often escaped him. Today, it was especially annoying because not only was the other man right but the situation wasn't funny. Not at all. The thought of Donovan with Iris made Tyler's blood run cold. Women flocked to the sales executive like bees to honey. What was the attraction? His bright hazel eyes, quick smile, natural charm? For Donovan, flirting was as easy as breathing. It had never been that simple for Tyler. How could Tyler compete with the other man?

Why am I so anxious to try?

"Aren't you dating someone?" Tyler's scowl deepened. How many women did Donovan need at one time?

"No, I'm not. In fact, I'm going through a dry spell."

"That's unusual." Almost unbelievable.

"Actually, it's not." Donovan's eyes twinkled as though he was laughing at Tyler. "I'm not the ladies' man you seem to think I am."

"I know." Tyler's words were almost grudging. Donovan wasn't a shallow, insincere cheat. He was just very popular. "Are you going to ask Iris out?"

"No, but obviously you should."

Tyler's pulse jumped. "Have you been playing me this entire time?"

"Of course I have."

So Donovan wasn't interested in Iris? *Great.* Not that it mattered. "It's not a good idea to mix business and pleasure."

Donovan flashed a grin. "Do your contradictions ever confuse you? Because they confuse me."

"Are you trying to be funny?"

"You design cutting-edge computer games with fake worlds that push the envelope. But your real life is very conservative."

"That's because it's real life, Van." Tyler's tone was dry. "There are consequences."

"I understand you don't want to start a personal relationship while you're working together." Donovan leaned into his desk toward Tyler. "But what about once the launch is over?"

"She probably won't be interested."

"Why not?"

Tyler hesitated. "Because I told her our company isn't a dating service."

Donovan closed his eyes briefly. "Tell me you didn't really say that."

"I wish I could."

Donovan sank back onto his chair. "Good Lord, Ty, you really *don't* know how to speak with women, do you?"

"Do you have a more helpful response?" Tyler's shoulders rose and fell with a deep breath.

"You need to work on your people skills."

"That's not much better." Tyler's gaze moved restlessly around his friend's office.

A stack of CDs stood on a shelf above Donovan's desk. It shared space with vacation photos and an older group shot taken after their college commencement ceremony. Donovan, Xavier and Tyler were lined up in their caps and gowns, flexing their biceps for the camera. On the desk beside his computer was a large framed photograph of a young Donovan with his mother.

"Ty, once in a while, you need to step away from your computer, and talk with real people." Donovan's advice reclaimed Tyler's attention.

"That's what everyone keeps telling me." Tyler sighed again.

"You should listen to us."

"What do I do in the meantime?" Discussing his concern with Iris had seemed like a good idea at the time. But judging by Iris's and Donovan's reactions, it had been the dumbest decision ever. How did he fix it?

"Start with an apology, then pray for the best." Donovan's tone implied Tyler didn't have a snowball's chance of coming out of this situation unscathed.

Tyler winced. The initial encounter already had cost him a couple of layers of skin. He rose from the chair. "I'll get started." But what should he pray for first? Forgiveness for the stupid remarks he'd made or a speedy and successful product launch so he could stop fighting the attraction he'd had since he first saw Iris?

■ ■ ■ ■

Tyler considered the closed and cautious expressions of the Anderson Adventures associates sitting stiffly in the lounge Wednesday morning. At least one representative from each of the company's five departments was present for the focus group: human resources, information technology, sales, product development and finance.

The room held a couple of gray sofas, matching armchairs, Maplewood coffee tables, laminate dining tables, a refrigerator and microwaves. Tyler chose a seat on one of the square gray armchairs behind a coffee table. He only half listened as Iris explained the purpose of the meeting. Judging by their body language, this morning promised to be an even worse experience than Monday's executive meeting. Tyler frowned again at the memory of his father second-guessing him.

A digital recorder sat on the coffee table, ready to document the session — if anyone spoke. He returned his attention to Iris, who stood about an arm's length from him on his left. She'd been cool toward him since the executive meeting Monday. He wasn't sure but he had a feeling she was still upset that he'd wrongfully accused her of flirting with Donovan. He knew now he'd been an idiot. How could he fix this?

"We want your candid input on this internal launch." She gestured toward him. "So just ignore Ty."

"That's hard to do." Ted Silvestri from the information technology department slid a blue-eyed glance toward Tyler before dropping his attention to the floor. "He's scowling at us."

Tyler met Iris's gaze, surprised. "Sorry."

Iris's concern morphed into humor. "Let's focus on the task at hand, shall we?" She turned back to their audience. "The internal product launch of 'Osiris's Journey' is first and foremost a celebration of you, and recognition of your contributions."

"Excuse me, Iris?" Sherry raised her hand. "I don't mean to sound as though I'm not a team player but I don't understand how the launch impacts me. I'm an administrative assistant. How did I contribute?"

"What contributions are you talking about?" Jarnett Smucker, director of human resources, asked. Behind large glasses, her small gray eyes were fixed on Iris. Her bright red hair sizzled from a bun on top of her head. "HR didn't work on the game.

The launch is only about production and sales."

Tyler studied the fifteen employees in front of him. *Did I hear them correctly?* "You're wrong." He rose from his seat, trying to work through his confusion. "Sherry, you schedule all our development meetings and verify the outside vendor invoices. Isn't that contributing to the product?"

Sherry's bright blue eyes widened. "I guess it is."

"You saved me a lot of time and trouble." Tyler rolled up the sleeves of his cream knit shirt. He approached Ren Komura from the purchasing department. The middle-aged man sat beside Sherry on one of the navy sofas. "Ren, you found the best distribution services at the best price for 'Osiris's Journey.' "

"That's right." Ren swept his straight raven hair back from his wide forehead. His dark eyes were cautious as they met Tyler's gaze. "I contacted several vendors to get a good bid."

"And we appreciate your efforts." Tyler looked to Jarnett. "HR is responsible for finding the best people for every position in our company. That's just one of your contributions to all of our games."

"Well, yes, that's true." Jarnett adjusted

her glasses.

Tyler stepped back, shoving his hands into the front pockets of his navy blue slacks. He made eye contact with the associates as he spoke. "I've worked beside most of you in every department of this company as I learned Anderson Adventures' operation. That's how I know that everyone contributes to the success of our products."

The silence was heavy as he returned to his chair. What were they thinking? Had his words even made a difference?

"Thank you for clarifying everyone's contributions, Ty." Iris's coffee eyes were warm with approval.

"Do those contributions include finance?" Lola Ray, an accountant, shifted on her chair. A blush warmed her brown skin.

"Just keep approving my budget requests." Tyler smiled.

Lola turned to Iris. "In that case, at the internal launch, I'd like a meal, preferably a buffet, with dessert."

Laughter filled the room and the atmosphere shifted. This was a new experience. He was connecting with the associates. Tension dissipated, his and theirs. Excitement and enthusiasm replaced it.

"Forget the food." Ted interjected. "A live band."

"We need to be sensitive to the budget," Lola cautioned. "We don't want this to be the company's one and only celebration for the year."

"Can we bring our families?" Ren directed his question to Tyler.

"I'm afraid not." Would his response dampen the enthusiasm? "For security reasons, this internal launch has to be associates only."

Everyone nodded their understanding except Jarnett. She crossed her arms. "Well, my husband will be very disappointed."

"You can bring him back a piece of cake." Sherry's tone was sincere, though her response elicited laughter. Tyler breathed easier.

Jarnett cut Sherry a glance. "It's not the same as attending the event."

Ted raised his hand. "A DJ?"

"Some form of music. Duly noted." The smile Iris offered Ted was almost as warm and bright as the one she'd given Donovan two days ago.

Tyler gritted his teeth. Iris smiled at everyone but him.

The Anderson Adventures associates continued to offer suggestions: off-site location with easy parking; demo of the computer game; half workday; buffet lunch;

minimal, if any, executive presentations. A little more than an hour later, the meeting ended on a high note.

After her closing comments, Iris gestured toward Tyler. "Is there anything you'd like to add?"

"Thanks for your time and input." To Tyler, the words weren't enough to convey his appreciation but the associates seemed satisfied. He exhaled. He'd survived his first associates meeting, though, technically, Iris had run the show. They made a good team.

"Thank you, Ty." Iris's nod indicated her approval. She turned back to the group. "If you have any other suggestions, please contact me. My email address is on the handout. Thanks for your time. Have a great day."

Muffled conversations faded away as the associates returned to their offices. The sense of excitement followed them from the lounge.

Tyler stood as Iris turned off the audio recorder and gathered her belongs. "Can I help?"

"I've got it." She didn't look at him. Was she still stewing over his comment about Donovan?

"How do you think the meeting went?"

"It went well." Iris led him from the room.

"More importantly, what do you think?"

"It was better than I'd expected." Tyler walked beside her. "Did you get the information you need?"

"I did." She looked up at him. "You did a good job, using your personal experience to explain everyone's role in product development. I was impressed."

"It was nothing." *Am I blushing?*

"Without your intervention, the meeting would've ended before it even began."

I'm definitely *blushing.*

Tyler had never blushed before in his life. First, he'd made a fool of himself over her smiling at Donovan. Now he was blushing like a schoolgirl.

What is she doing to me?

"Glad to help." Tyler stepped aside to let her take the staircase first. Her fragrance touched him as she walked by. Tyler's gaze strayed to her long well-shaped legs as they climbed from the second floor to the fifth-floor executive offices.

Iris's voice broke his trance. "I'll incorporate their wish list into our plans."

"How many of those things will fit into our budget?"

"All of them." She tossed him a look over her shoulder, part mischief and all confidence.

Tyler stilled on the staircase. That look squeezed his heart and caused his pulse to speed up.

He caught up with Iris at the top of the staircase. "We need to keep the event on-site. We can't risk having information about the computer game leak before our official launch."

Iris stopped close enough for Tyler to catch another intoxicating breath of her fragrance. "Hosting the event off-site would make it seem more special."

"It's too risky." Tyler reached past her to open the main door to the executive offices.

"All right." She sounded disappointed by his decision. "I should have the estimate to you by a week from Friday." Iris turned toward the reception area and smiled. "Hi, Sherry. Thanks again for organizing the focus group and for participating in it."

"It was fun." Sherry turned to Tyler. "I hadn't realized you'd worked in every department in the company. That's impressive."

"Told you," Iris whispered before disappearing down the hall. Did her teasing remark mean she'd forgiven him for the accusation he'd made Monday?

Tyler's gaze moved over her glossy sable hair floating just above her narrow shoulders to her slender hips swinging hypnotically beneath her A-line red skirt. Her matching red stilettos were silent on the silver-and-black carpet but his pulse beat with every step she took.

"Is there anything I can do for you, Ty?" The knowing look in Sherry's bright blue eyes caused his cheeks to heat again.

"No, but thanks, Sherry." Tyler walked away.

He needed to pull himself together. If other people noticed his attraction to his marketing consultant, he was in trouble.

Back in his office, Tyler dropped onto his black leather executive chair and logged on to his computer. He stared blankly at his screen.

Two days ago, he'd given Iris a pompous lecture about pursuing romantic entanglements at Anderson Adventures. Maybe he should have delivered his speech to the mirror instead.

"May I come in?" Hours later, Foster stood in the threshold of Tyler's office.

Despite having been hard at work for the past four hours, his father still looked crisp in his white shirt, gold tie and dark gray pants. He carried his matching suit jacket in the crook of his arm.

Tyler checked his wristwatch. It was after noon. He'd lost almost three hours since the morning's focus group meeting. How had that happened?

"Of course." He locked his computer screen, then swiveled his seat to face his father on the other side of his desk.

"I'd expected you to come to my office after your meeting this morning." Foster settled his jacket on the back of one of the visitor's chairs. He lowered himself onto the other.

"I thought I was handling this project myself." Tyler searched Foster's eyes. Why was his father checking up on him?

"You are. But that doesn't mean you shouldn't keep me apprised." Foster propped his elbows on the chair's arms and linked his fingers together. "How did it go?"

"It went well." Tyler settled back on his chair, forcing himself to relax. "We got a lot of good participation."

"You can give me details." Foster's faint smile teased him. "I'm on the list of associates who are cleared to receive such sensitive information."

"I'm sorry." Tyler grinned at his father's words. "I'm not used to talking about my projects in such depth."

"That's one of the things we're trying to

113

change."

Tyler folded his hands on his desk and collected his thoughts. "It seems Iris was right. Everyone was excited about the internal launch."

"I heard they weren't at first."

Tyler stilled. Foster's response could mean only one thing. "Did Iris brief you on the meeting?"

"She answered a few questions — after I asked her." Foster cocked his head. "Did you think she was here to spy on you?"

"I don't understand why you spoke with her first."

"I wouldn't have had to seek her out if you'd given me an update. I'm still in charge, Ty."

"Understood, sir."

"Iris isn't spying on you or undermining your leadership. In fact, according to her, you saved the meeting. She was quite impressed with you."

That annoying heat inched up his neck again. The thought of Iris praising him made him feel like a rock star. Was he ridiculous to react that way? "I'm glad everything worked out."

"I thought you didn't want to discuss the meeting with me because it had gone badly."

The truth was Tyler hadn't given a thought

to briefing his father. He'd been too distracted by Iris and the cold shoulder she'd given him all day. He wasn't going to admit that, though. Ever.

"No, the meeting went well. Of course, everyone had a different opinion."

"Such as?"

"Some people want the launch during the day. Others want it after work. Some want breakfast, others want lunch. We heard requests for an off-site location. A few want it here. Someone asked whether family members could attend —"

"We can't invite anyone from outside of the company. There's too much risk of a leak, intentionally or not."

"I agree. That's why I told Iris to keep the launch on-site."

Foster looked confused. "Why?"

Tyler frowned. "To prevent information about the game getting out before our external launch."

"We're not going to discuss product specifications in detail. The event is about having fun."

"But we're going to discuss game features."

"I don't want the internal launch to happen here." Foster's tone was firm. "We'll include a nondisclosure agreement in the venue contract."

Tyler searched his father's aquiline features. Foster was second-guessing him. Again. "I thought you wanted me to lead the launch."

"I do."

"And I don't think we should take it off-site. It's too risky."

"We agreed this launch would be extraordinary." Foster spread his hands. "The lounge, which is the only space in this building large enough for a company meeting, is not extraordinary."

Tyler swallowed a sigh. "All right. I'll ask Iris to get an estimate for holding the event offsite."

"Remember, we wouldn't have the successes we've had without our associates. Ordinary isn't good enough." Foster pushed himself from the chair. "I'd better get moving. I'm meeting Kayla for lunch."

"Give her my love."

"I will." Foster turned toward the door.

This was the second time his father had second-guessed a decision he'd made. First, Foster had voted against his idea of keeping the product launches simple. Now he wanted to hold the internal launch off-site even though an outside venue made them more vulnerable to information leaks. How many more times were they going to butt heads?

But, on a positive note, Iris had given him a good review when she'd discussed the focus-group meeting with Foster. Tyler's tension eased slightly. Her praise probably had given him bonus points with his father. It also showed that even when she was annoyed with him, she'd still treat him fairly.

CHAPTER 6

"And then he said, 'I want to be clear that you're here for the product launch — and that's all.' " Iris deepened her voice to imitate Tyler. Their confrontation had taken place two days earlier but she was still fuming over his accusation.

The salmon and broiled asparagus Lily had made for their weekly family dinner on Wednesday were forgotten for the moment. Her two older sisters sat on the other side of their family's dining table, now Lily's table. Iris waited for their reactions.

Rose's wide cocoa eyes narrowed dangerously. "Is he crazy?"

Lily blinked. "Was he serious?"

"I couldn't believe it, either." Iris chased an asparagus spear across her plate.

"Men." Rose sounded as though the word left a bad taste in her mouth. "They think they know everything when in fact, they know nothing."

Here we go again.

"Could we please not make this about you and Ben?" Iris asked, referring to Rose's ex-fiancé, Benjamin Shippley.

"Iris!" Lily sent a worried look toward Rose.

"Did I say anything about him?" Rose stiffened.

"You were thinking him." Iris cut into the salmon. It sliced like butter. Pity her appetite was gone. "Ben was a jerk but do you still have to be so negative?"

"Compared to you, everyone is negative." Rose glared across the table. "Take off your rose-tinted glasses, Pollyanna. Ty's comment shows he doesn't trust you."

"He will once he gets to know me." Iris claimed a piece of salmon with her fork.

"No, he won't because he doesn't want to trust you." Rose raised her voice.

"You're assuming that, like you, Ty doesn't trust anyone." Iris held Rose's darkening gaze. "I don't believe that."

"We're on your side, Iris." Lily's voice was strained. "His comment was uncalled for."

"You don't think I can convince him to trust me, either?" Iris struggled with a sense of betrayal.

"You shouldn't have to." Lily's whiskey gaze was intent. "The question isn't whether you can convince Tyler to trust you. Why doesn't he trust you now?"

Good question. "I don't know."

Tyler had been such a jerk Monday to imply she'd behaved unprofessionally by smiling at his friend. But during the meeting this morning, he'd seemed like a different person. When he'd stood to explain to his associates how they'd individually contributed to the company's success, she'd seen the good in him. He'd been thoughtful and charming.

How do I get him to be thoughtful and charming to me?

"He doesn't trust you because he's a man." Rose stabbed an asparagus spear with her fork and shoved it into her mouth. "They aren't trustworthy so they assume no one else is, either."

"All men aren't bad." Regret weighed on Iris. Would Rose ever believe that again?

"Don't let Ben win." Lily's voice was soft but firm.

Iris's heart squeezed at the pain that flashed across Rose's elegant, honey features. "Lil's right, Rosie. Ben was an ass. There's someone out there who'll give you the love and loyalty you deserve."

"For how long?" Rose lowered her fork and leaned into the table. "I was with Ben for two years before I realized he'd been cheating on me almost from the start. Love is a lie."

Iris again fantasized about pummeling her sister's ex-fiancé. "I don't believe that. I'm looking forward to meeting Mr. Right and living happily ever after. What about you, Lil?"

Lily seemed startled. "I haven't thought about it. I've had other things on my mind."

"Like what?" Iris sipped her cucumber water. It was the first time Lily had made the beverage. It wasn't that bad.

"Just other things." Lily shrugged. "My career for example. I'm not looking for love. If it happens, it happens. In the meantime, I'm busy living my life."

Iris was impatient with Lily's philosophical attitude. "Don't you want someone to share your busy life with?" She sounded wistful even to her own ears. "Someone to plan your evening with or to be spontaneous with?"

Rose snorted. "Someone whose schedule conflicts with yours. Someone you have to compromise with every time there's a decision to make."

Iris gave her older sister a pointed look. "Someone who cheers you up when you're in a bad mood."

Rose was stubborn. "Someone who leaves the toilet seat up or squeezes the toothpaste from the middle of the tube."

Lily gave Rose another concerned look. "Perhaps we should change the subject."

Iris was more than willing to comply. "What should I do about Ty? Should I confront him, ask him why he doesn't trust me?"

"Why? So he could lie to you?" Rose snorted.

Lily shook her head. "Just be aware that you're at a disadvantage. You'll have to be extra careful and triple-check your work."

"Why should she have to work that way?" Rose pointed at Iris with her fork. "If I were you, I'd march into his office and tell him what he could do with his suspicious, little mind."

"I need the money, Rose." *And the campaign is exciting — not to mention Tyler himself, even if he is infuriating.* "Regardless of what the two of you think, I believe I can change his mind about me."

Was that challenge part of Tyler's appeal? There was something undeniably compelling about Anderson Adventures' vice president of product development. He challenged her — and infuriated her. He made her heart beat faster.

"Good luck with that." Rose ate a forkful of salmon.

Iris smiled at her sister's sarcasm. "I have the skills to prove you wrong."

"I believe in you, Iris." Rose's voice was somber. "It's your client I don't trust."

Maybe she was being foolishly optimistic. But despite her annoyance over Tyler's comment, she was confident he'd treat her fairly, unlike her previous employer.

With or without her rose-tinted glasses, she'd gain his trust. She needed it for this product launch. And she wanted it for something more that she wasn't prepared to accept. Not yet.

"Hard at work, Ty?" Lauren's greeting interrupted Tyler's train of thought.

With great reluctance, Tyler saved the file on his computer screen and rose to his feet. "Hello, Lauren."

Why had she come to his office and how long was she planning to stay?

"You look busy." But rather than walking away, Lauren stepped into his office.

"There's a lot to do." And he was running out of time. "Are you meeting Xavier for lunch?"

Tyler checked his watch. It was a few minutes after noon on the second Thursday in April. He had an appointment with Iris in about three hours to discuss the internal launch. His excitement over their upcoming meeting was out of character. He usually did everything he could to avoid them. But in this case, he actually looked forward to the excuse to spend time with her.

"Yes, but I thought I'd stop by to say hello." Lauren came to a stop in front of his desk.

Really? When did we become friends? Tyler mentally shrugged. He'd play along. "How are you?"

"Fine." Lauren's smile was stiff. "How's the product launch progressing?"

"It's going well." Tyler shoved his hands into the front pockets of his beige khakis, hoping to mask his impatience.

Lauren had accessorized her pale blue business dress with a chunky silver necklace and matching bracelet. Her sleek brown bob ended just above her shoulders. What did Xavier see in the corporate executive? Yes, she was beautiful, intelligent, poised and professional. But she also was cold and distant. He couldn't imagine Lauren engaging Anderson Adventures' associates in the recent focus group the way Iris had.

"You have a lot riding on the launch's success." Lauren rested a hip against one of the guest chairs and slid her gaze around his office.

"There's a lot riding on every product launch." Tyler resisted the urge to check the time again. How long was it going to take her to say hello?

Lauren's apparent interest in developing a better relationship with Xavier's family and learning more about their business was understandable. But he didn't have time for idle chitchat. The release date for "Osiris's Journey" was coming up fast — thirteen weeks and counting — and they still had a lot of features to refine.

"But you're in charge of this launch." Lauren kept talking. "If it fails, your father will look elsewhere for the company's next CEO."

"How do you know that?" Tyler's brows knitted.

"You, Xavier and Van discussed it, remember?" Lauren adjusted the strap of her black purse on her shoulder, then rested her well-manicured hands on the back of a guest chair. "I overheard you."

Tyler's memory flashed back to the afternoon Lauren had walked into his office while he'd been telling Donovan and Xavier about his meeting with his father. Was she in the habit of eavesdropping outside offices?

"We have a good product. The launch will be successful." Tyler needed an interruption to allow him to gracefully get out of spending any more time with Lauren.

"I'm sure you'll do your best."

"Thanks." Had she meant to sound condescending?

"The internal launch is Friday, May first, right? I'm sorry I won't be allowed to attend it." Lauren's gaze never wavered from his. "Xavier said you aren't inviting guests to the event."

"It's for associates only."

"That's what he said." Lauren shrugged a thin shoulder. "I admit that I'm disappointed."

"I'm sure you can understand. It's an internal event." Why were they having this conversation?

"Will your aunt be there?"

"Of course."

Lauren arched a perfectly plucked eyebrow. "So you're making an exception for her?"

"Aunt Kayla is a member of the executive team." Tyler was approaching the end of his patience.

"And she's family. I've been dating your

cousin for some time now. I feel like a part of your family."

But you're not. And you've only been dating Xavier for two months.

Tyler glanced at his monitor, choosing not to address Lauren's point. "I'd better get back to work. As I said, there's a lot to do."

"By all means." Lauren stepped back from the chair. "You're welcome to join us for lunch."

No way. "Thanks but I'm working through."

Lauren's smile was almost sincere. "Once in a while, you should try getting away from your desk."

"That's what Xavier and Van say." And his father. And Aunt Kayla and Sherry.

"They're right." Lauren turned and disappeared through his doorway.

Tyler returned to his seat. But he wasn't able to refocus on his product testing. Instead, he stared blindly at his monitor. Why had Lauren come to see him? What did she want? There was something disconcerting about Lauren. He couldn't define it. But whatever it was made him uncomfortable around her.

Iris posed a completely different problem. There was something about his marketing consultant that compelled him to seek her out. She ruled his thoughts from the moment he opened his eyes in the morning until he settled into bed at night. What was it? And what could he do to fight it?

He'd thought having her nearby would dim her appeal. He'd been wrong. More than two weeks had passed since she'd moved into the small conference room down the hall and around the corner from his office. During that time, his attraction to her had only strengthened. He was going out of his mind.

Tyler's stomach growled. Loudly. According to the time displayed in the lower corner of his computer monitor, he'd been woolgathering for almost five minutes. No, not woolgathering. Iris had consumed his thoughts again. He frowned at the minifridge in the far corner of his office. He'd packed a perfectly decent sandwich and container of soup but they didn't interest him.

What was Iris doing for lunch? She had a habit of eating at her desk, too. He'd see her using the microwave in the office kitchenette. Tyler tapped his keyboard to lock his computer, then pushed himself to his feet. He had an urge to find Iris. This time, he wouldn't fight it.

He left his office, closing the door so the

automatic lock triggered. He strode down the hall to the small conference room and found its door locked. Tyler knocked to get Iris's attention. She rose from her seat.

Iris pulled open the door. "Hello, Ty."

Her dark purple business dress skimmed her neat, slender curves, stopping just above her knees. The color made her honey features seem even warmer. Her matching three-inch stilettos caused his brain to stutter. *How many shoes does she own?*

Tyler looked into her cool coffee eyes. She still hadn't forgiven him. "You can prop open the door."

"I suppose I could." Iris stepped back.

Tyler dropped to his left knee. He reached for the wedge of oak wood to push it beneath the door just as Iris extended her leg to tap the wood into place. He caught hold of her ankle. Tyler's arm shook as though he'd been jolted with electricity. The warmth of her skin filled the palm of his hand. His gaze followed the length of her long, well-curved calf to her knee. His hand itched to trace the shapely muscle. Dazed, he looked up, still on one knee. Iris's beautiful eyes were clouded. She tugged her leg from his hand. Embarrassed, Tyler let her go.

"Is this the part where you ask me to try

on a glass slipper?" Her teasing smile trembled around the edges.

Tyler shoved the wedge under the door, then rose to his feet. He drew in a breath, capturing the scent of citrus and vanilla. Iris's scent. "Am I your Prince Charming?"

Iris's thoughts scattered to the four winds. Had Tyler Anderson just turned the tables on her? She'd expected him to respond to her comment with a blank stare. Instead he'd issued his own challenge. She'd underestimated him — and the effect of his smooth baritone on her senses. Not to mention the feel of his hand on her leg.

"Our meeting isn't until later this afternoon." Iris retreated to her desk. Her ankle was still warm from his touch. "I haven't crunched the estimates from all of the vendors yet."

"How's it looking so far?"

Iris stopped beside her chair. She dragged her gaze from Tyler to the papers strewn across the glass-topped table. "So far, it's even better than I'd hoped."

"Is there anything you can tell me now?" Tyler took a step toward the table. Then another. His movements were like a panther stalking his prey. Iris was mesmerized.

What were they talking about again? The

budget; that's right. "I can only speak in generalities. When we meet later this afternoon, I'll give you specific numbers."

"Fair enough." Tyler nodded toward the dark purple jacket hooked to the back of one of the chairs. "Let's get lunch."

"I brought my lunch." That was a lame response but he'd caught her by surprise.

"Eat it for dinner instead or lunch tomorrow."

Iris started to decline his invitation but the challenge in his eyes made her hesitate. "I don't know if that's such a good idea. All I did was smile at Donovan and you accused me of flirting with him. If I have lunch with you, what will you accuse me of?"

"Very good judgment." The gleam in his eyes caused Iris to doubt his claim.

"You usually work through lunch."

"So do you. But I've been told that I should see the world outside my desk once in a while. Join me." His voice evoked thoughts of something other than lunch.

What's going on here?

Iris glanced at the small silver cooler that held her chicken salad and thermos of iced tea. They'd both keep. Still she hesitated. His invitation was tempting but she couldn't afford to give in to what she suspected was a growing attraction to her client. Iris wanted to fall in love. But this was not the right place and certainly not the right time.

She tightened her grip on the back of her chair. "I really should keep working."

"I admire your dedication but you could use a break."

Careful, Iris, he's not playing fair. Remember Cathy's words of caution. But another voice whispered, *You started your own firm during an economic recession. When have you ever allowed caution to be your guide?*

"All right." Iris drew a deep breath, then collected her jacket from a nearby chair. "Let's do lunch."

The approval in his gaze made her question her sanity. Less than twenty minutes later, they were shown to a booth at a neighborhood restaurant. The young hostess gave them each a menu. Then Jan, their server, arrived to take their drink orders, two ice waters with lemon.

Iris lifted her gaze from her menu. "Why did you invite me to lunch?" A better question was why had she accepted? She wasn't ready to answer that question, though.

"We eat at our desks too often. I thought we could both use a change." His shrug was a small movement of broad muscles under his beige jersey.

"If I'd invited you to lunch, would you

have accused me of flirting with you?"

"You're still upset over my comment about your smiling at Van."

He was intuitive for a computer geek. "It was offensive."

"You're right. I'm sorry. I was wrong." He sounded as if he really meant it.

"All right." She'd never expected him to apologize, especially not so easily. Now that he'd removed her resentment, she felt naked in front of him.

Moments later, Jan returned with their drinks and took their meal orders. Iris requested the salmon salad. Tyler asked for a Caesar salad and a burger.

Iris gazed around the restaurant. She'd never been here before. Their surroundings looked expensive, dark wood and black leather. Comfortable booths circled the room. Tables were arranged in the center with plenty of space for the waitstaff to wind their way across the floor. The wood-paneled walls were decorated with black-and-white photos of Columbus. The effect was a warm neighborhood ambience.

"What do you have so far for the internal launch budget?" Tyler asked.

"I haven't finished compiling the vendor estimates yet. We're supposed to meet this afternoon."

"Then what would you like to talk about?" Tyler leaned into the table.

Is he flirting with me?

Iris's protective instincts kicked in. "You have a point." She drank her water as she collected her thoughts. "I was able to negotiate with the vendors to get all of your employees' requests for the event."

Tyler's eyebrows rose. "Even Ted's live band?"

"He agreed to a disc jockey, remember?"

"That's right. Good work." The approval in Tyler's dark eyes caused the pulse at the base of Iris's throat to beat wildly.

"Thank you." She sipped her water.

"Today's April ninth." Tyler sat back on his chair. "The event's only a month away. Will that be enough time?"

You still don't trust me to deliver. "It's three weeks and one day away. I've put a hold on the car service and convention center ballroom. All you need to do is sign the contracts, if you agree with them."

"I'll look at them when we meet later. Have you worked with these companies before?"

She had. Iris told Tyler about her past projects with the car-service company and her contact at the city's convention center. His questions kept Iris on her toes. At the same time, the attention he focused on her was almost seductive. She struggled to concentrate.

Their conversation was interrupted when Jan brought their lunches and again when she refilled their water glasses.

"Take me through the schedule." Tyler started with his salad. "What time will the event start?"

Without her project folder, Iris worked from memory. Not a problem. She'd been reviewing the information all morning. "The car service will send drivers to Anderson Adventures at 10:00 a.m. Your employees will settle into the ballroom. Your father will greet them and start the event with a brief speech. Then the convention center's wait-staff will serve lunch."

"Why would we feed them before the presentations?" Tyler ate more of his salad.

Iris watched Tyler carry a forkful of lettuce to his mouth and slip it between his lips. She swallowed. Hard. "Your associates will be more attentive on a full stomach. Trust me."

What's *wrong with me? I've had business lunches before. Why am I finding it so hard to concentrate with this man?*

Iris tried to collect her thoughts as she nudged a tomato to the edge of her plate, then sliced the salmon and salad in her bowl.

"Good point." Tyler nodded, holding her gaze.

Is he aware of the effect he has on me? Please don't let him know Donovan's not the one on my mind. He is.

Iris rushed to fill the silence. "Speaking of presentations, how's yours coming?"

"I'll have it for you before lunch tomorrow."

What was taking him so long?

Iris wanted Tyler to trust her to make the internal and external launches a success but she was a bundle of nerves herself. She'd feel a heck of a lot better with his presentation in hand. It was the main feature of the entire event.

"Has my father given you his speech?" Tyler bit into his burger.

"Yes, it's really good."

"I'm sure it is." There was an odd note in his voice.

"I had very few comments. I'll send my feedback to both of you by the end of the day for a final review."

"I'd like to see it first."

"Sure." Iris angled her head. Curiosity gave her something to concentrate on other than her uncomfortable attraction. "May I ask why?"

"Don't worry. I'm not putting you in the middle of a controversy." Tyler took another drink of water. "I just want to make sure my father and I aren't repeating each other."

He sounded reasonable. *Then why do I feel like he isn't telling me everything?*

"Is it true you're in line to succeed your father as CEO of Anderson Adventures — providing he's happy with the way you handle the launches?"

"Where did you hear that?" Tyler seemed tense.

Iris lowered her knife and fork. "Please don't misunderstand. Your associates weren't gossiping. They asked how the internal launch was progressing. That's when they expressed their concern over the company's future."

"They must be very comfortable with you to confide in you." He sounded surprised.

"Are the rumors true?"

"Yes. Why?"

Talk about pressure. "We both have a lot riding on this project, which is the reason we need to be honest with each other."

"Agreed."

Iris smiled. He sounded so much like his father when he said that. "Good. You can start by telling me the real reason you want to see Foster's talking points first."

Tyler put down what remained of his burger. "You really aren't like any consultant I've ever worked with before."

"Is that a good thing?"

"I have a feeling you think you're in charge."

"No, I don't." *Do I?* Iris ignored the warmth in her cheeks. "Just tell me why there's tension between you and your father."

Tyler arched an eyebrow. "No, you don't think you're in charge. Not at all." There was irony in his voice. "I love my father very much but he keeps second-guessing my decisions."

"He has very definite opinions about the launch. But he's the CEO." Iris smiled to soften her words. "I'm sure the fact he's your father adds to his certainty that he knows best."

"It's my launch. He should leave the decisions to me." Tyler dragged a hand over his close-cropped hair.

"Tell him that," Iris suggested. "If your promotion depends on how you handle this project, then tell him you want to have total control over it. You want to fail or succeed on our own."

Iris finished her salad while Tyler digested

her words.

Finally, he nodded his agreement. "I'll take your advice. Thanks."

"You're welcome." She smiled, thinking of Rose. "I have some experience handling bossy relatives."

Tyler's eyes widened. "Someone bossier than you? That's hard to imagine."

Iris's lips curved into a lopsided smile. "I never said I listened to her."

"That sounds like the woman I'm getting to know."

Iris's gaze slid away from the admiration in Tyler's dark eyes. She was getting to know him, as well. It scared her how much she liked what she saw.

CHAPTER 7

"Are we on schedule with the internal launch?" Foster stood in the threshold of Tyler's office.

It was almost six o'clock Friday evening — a day after his lunch with Iris. Anderson Adventures was as still and quiet as a morgue. Even Donovan and Xavier had left for the weekend. Tyler was pretty sure he and his father were the last people in the office. Judging by the black faux-leather briefcase in Foster's fist, Tyler was about to become the last executive standing.

"I signed the vendor contracts yesterday." Tyler saved his computer file, then swung his chair around to face his father.

"I would've liked to have seen them." Foster strolled into Tyler's office and sat in front of his desk. He placed his briefcase beside the chair. Foster had paired his conservative brown suit with a bold red tie. It was a sharp if old-fashioned look.

"These weren't the first contracts I've reviewed." Tyler tried not to sound defensive.

"I know." Foster adjusted the crease in his suit pants before crossing his legs. "In the future, let me know if you want me to review anything with you. How are things going with Iris?"

"Fine." He welcomed his father's change of subject. "I like the communication pieces she's creating for us."

"She's doing good work." Foster nodded. "The two of you had lunch yesterday."

"How did you know that?"

Foster chuckled. "I saw you leaving together. I like her. She has a lot of spirit and determination."

Yes, she does. She's intelligent, creative and sexy as hell. But Tyler didn't want his growing attraction to their marketing consultant to bias him toward her work. "Let's see how well the launches go."

"I've been thinking about the internal launch." Foster rested his elbows on the arms of his chair and linked his fingers. "Our associates should meet us at the convention center instead of driving to the office, then taking limos to the center."

His father was second-guessing him. Again. "Are you concerned about the cost?"

"No, you and Xavier have assured me that Iris's initial estimates are within your comfort zone." Foster arched a brow. "Considering how stingy the two of you can be, I'm certain we're nowhere near overspending."

"If it's not about the expense, why do you want to change the transportation arrangements?"

"It'll be more convenient for our associates to drive themselves to the convention center."

This again? They'd had this debate last week. He'd thought it had been decided. Why was Foster revisiting it?

Foster spread his hands. "We shouldn't make them drive all the way into the office."

"We're not forcing them to do that." Tyler leaned into his desk. "We're offering the limo as an option. It'll save them the hassle of driving downtown and the expense of parking at the center."

Foster hesitated. "I don't want anyone to feel pressured into coming to the office first."

"We'll make it clear that they have a choice."

"Good, then." Foster started to push

himself to his feet. "I'll let you get back to work."

"Dad, wait. There's something I've been meaning to ask you."

"What is it?" Foster resumed his seat.

Tyler recalled Iris's theory on Foster's possible motivation for second-guessing him. Her opinion was a good place to start. "I realize that as CEO, it's hard for you to step back and let someone else take the lead on a project. Being my father, as well, must make it even harder. But, Dad, I need to do this on my own without being second-guessed."

"I'm just trying to help, Ty."

"I know and although I appreciate your input, I want to succeed or fail without your shadow looming over me."

Foster was silent for a moment, watching Tyler from the other side of the desk. The silence seemed to go on for an hour but probably was only a few seconds. "You're right, son. I'll back off."

"Thanks for understanding." That was easier than he'd imagined it would be. He was glad he'd told his father how he felt — and grateful that Iris had suggested it.

"I wouldn't have imagined us having this conversation a month ago. I'm pleased and proud that you proved me wrong."

"Thanks, Dad."

"By the way, how's your speech coming along?"

Tyler swallowed a sigh. His father was still checking up on him.

"It's getting there." That was an overstatement. He hadn't even started it. But, according to Iris's production schedule, the executive team was supposed to get Foster's and Tyler's speeches on Monday to review and provide. *Panic.*

"I'm looking forward to reading it." Foster stood. "Don't stay too late."

"I won't." Tyler held his smile until his father disappeared down the hall.

I'm doomed.

He had two days to put together a fifteen-minute presentation but he didn't even know where to start. Communication had never been his strength. He needed help.

Forty minutes later, Tyler hesitated in front of Iris's door. It was early April but the weather refused to show even a promise of spring. A cool breeze tugged at his steel-gray overcoat as though nudging him away from Iris's townhome. Mother Nature had a point. The last time Tyler had shown up uninvited and unannounced, Iris had been irritated. Actually, that was an understatement.

He shoved his hands deep into his pockets and took a step back. Maybe he should call Donovan. Words came easily to the vice president of sales. No. His shoulders rose and fell in frustration. His presentation for the internal launch was about more than words. Iris was the only one who understood that. She could get from him what he needed to express. Tyler gathered his courage, stepped forward and pressed her doorbell — quickly before doubts grabbed him again.

Less than a minute later, Iris appeared in the doorway. Irritation rose like steam in her coffee-colored eyes. "You're making a huge assumption about my personal life."

"Excuse me?" He hadn't expected that greeting. *Did I miss something?*

"What makes you think I'm alone? I could have company."

He felt sick. "Do you?"

"No, but I could have." She crossed her arms, drawing Tyler's attention to her loose-fitting dark purple jersey. Her normally sleek sable hair was tousled. Her elegant honey features were washed clean of cosmetics, making her look even younger. Her skimpy, pale gray shorts revealed long, well-shaped legs. Her toenails were painted a pale shade of pink that reminded him of cotton candy. The polished professional he'd been working with for the past two weeks had vanished. In her place was a woman who aroused his interest in things other than Anderson Adventures.

Tyler lifted both hands, palms out. "I know you don't hold client meetings in your home but I really need your help."

With those words, the irritation cleared from Iris's eyes. She stepped back, pulling the door wider. "Come in."

Tyler entered her townhome before she reconsidered. "Thank you."

She extended her hand for his coat, then hung it in her closet before leading him farther into her home. "What can I help you with?"

She'd cranked up the heat, which explained those short shorts despite the cool air outside. The savory scent of well-seasoned chicken accompanied Tyler through her living room and into her dining room. His gaze followed Iris as she crossed the entrance to her kitchen.

"Am I interrupting your dinner?" Tyler watched her stop in front of her stove and turn up the burner under the skillet.

"As a matter of fact, you are. Have you

eaten?" Iris picked up a knife and a carrot that lay beside a bowl of salad on the counter. From a CD player on the other end of the stone surface, Alicia Keys was singing about someone's smile.

"No, I came here straight from the office." Tyler's stomach growled as he watched Iris slice carrots into the bowl.

"I'm not making anything special. It's just chicken salad." She spoke with her back to him. "But there's enough for two."

"I don't want to put you to any trouble."

"Then we should've had this conversation at the office." Iris turned off the stove. She opened an overhead cabinet and pulled down two large bowls. "Since you're here, have a seat and tell me how I can help you."

Tyler pulled out a chair from under the matching mahogany dining table and settled onto it. "My father asked about the launch's progress this afternoon. He brought up having associates drive to the center again."

"That's not a good idea." Iris carried two tall glasses of ice water to the dining table.

"Agreed." Tyler spotted navy blue mats in the center of the table and slid them into place. "I took your advice and told him I wanted to succeed or fail on my own."

"What did he say?" Iris returned to the kitchen.

"He agreed. Then he asked to see my speech for the employee launch."

"I'd like to see it, too." Iris came back with two bowls of chicken salad. She set one in front of Tyler, then took her seat with the other. "It's due Monday."

"I'm having trouble with it." Tyler inhaled the savory scent of the chicken. His mouth watered.

"Most of your presentation is a demonstration of the game." Iris forked up her salad. "How much of it have you written?"

Tyler hesitated. "None."

Iris froze with her fork halfway to her mouth. She lowered her hand and faced him. "You told me you were working on it."

"I am. I just haven't written anything down."

"It's been two weeks. If you were having trouble, you should have said something before."

She was right. "I've been busy with the game's testing and modifications."

"You were also supposed to be busy writing this speech." Iris rose from the table. "Excuse me."

Tyler watched her leave the room, then heard her footsteps as she went upstairs. Where was she going? What was she doing?

He stared at his salad. Tension had a negative effect on his appetite.

Iris returned minutes later with a writing tablet and a ballpoint pen. She laid the materials next to Tyler before reclaiming her seat. "This will be a working dinner."

Tyler uncapped the pen. "Where do I start?"

"Where do you want to start?" Iris chewed a mouthful of salad. She would have made a tough teacher, the type students dreaded because she wouldn't give an inch.

"How about, 'This is a proud moment for Anderson Adventures'?"

Iris's dark eyes glazed over. "May I make a suggestion?"

"Please."

"When we held the focus group with fifteen of your associates, most of them said they didn't know how they played a part in 'Osiris's Journey.' "

"I remember." Tyler brought the meeting to mind. "The only ones who felt they'd contributed were the ones who'd directly worked on it."

"Use your speech to explain to the entire company how they've all contributed. Hearing that from you would mean a lot to them."

Tyler leaned back onto his chair. He was

more at ease than he'd been for the past two weeks. He hadn't even realized how much stress he'd been feeling over this speech. He'd just kept pushing it to the back of his mind. That's how he'd run out of time, though he'd never admit that to Iris.

Relief brought forth a smile. "I can do that."

They spent the next hour drafting the presentation and eating dinner. Tyler set the tone. Iris's encouragement came in the form of comments like "good idea" or "be more specific" or "seriously?" She made him laugh. He had almost as much fun writing this speech as he'd had designing the game — and it was all because of Iris.

She stood from the table. "Do you want more water?"

"I'll get it." Tyler filled their glasses from the filtered water section on her refrigerator, then brought them back.

"Thank you." Iris accepted her glass from him.

"Thank *you*." Tyler sat. "I couldn't have written this presentation without you."

"They're your words."

"But you helped me find them." Tyler watched a blush rise in Iris's cheeks. *Lovely.* "Just like you helped me find a way to talk to my father."

"As I said, I've been there myself."

"I've worked with you for two weeks but I don't know much about you." Tyler leaned into the table to get closer to her. "Who wants to be in charge of your family? Is it your father?"

"My parents are dead."

"I'm sorry."

"So am I." Iris's voice was soft. "My oldest sister is the bossy one. She thinks she's my mother. She always has."

"That must be difficult."

"I think it's hardest on my other sister." Iris sounded pensive. "She's in the middle, literally. She's always been the peacekeeper."

"So you have two sisters, no brothers?"

"That's right."

"Xavier and I are only children, but we grew up like brothers."

"When I first met your executive team, I could tell your family is very close. Even Van seems like an Anderson."

"Xavier and I met Van in college. He fit right in."

"I can tell." Iris reached for his dishes.

Tyler caught her wrist to stop her. He felt her pulse jump against his fingertips. "Let me clean up. It'll be my way of thanking you for dinner and for the overtime."

"Thanks aren't necessary." She arched a

brow. "As for the overtime, I charge a lot more than a few washed dishes."

"You can send me your bill." Tyler collected her setting, as well, and carried everything to her sink.

"I'll load the dishwasher later." Iris trailed him to the kitchen and leaned against the wall.

"I should get going so you can start your weekend." Tyler turned and was struck by those beautiful big eyes gazing at him.

"It won't be much of a weekend. I need to catch up on all the work I couldn't do during the week since a demanding client wants me to work from his office." Her smile softened the scold.

"If you're trying to make me feel bad, it's not working." Tyler stepped toward her. Only an arm's length separated them. "But I am curious. Why are you spending your Friday night alone?"

"Why are you fixated on my love life?"

"I'm not." He suddenly felt like the awkward teen he'd been: founder, president and sole member of his high school's computer club. The credential hadn't made him popular with the girls in his school.

Iris straightened from the wall and paced away from him. "First you warned me not to use Anderson Adventures for hookups."

"That's not what I said."

"Now you want to know why I don't have a date on a Friday night." Iris stopped beside the table. "You sound pretty fixated to me."

"I didn't mean to offend you. I'm just curious." *Curious about everything to do with you.*

"Why?"

He should never have said anything. "I would've thought a woman like you would have men breaking down her door."

"A woman like me?"

"You know what you look like." Tyler gestured toward her. "You're beautiful. You're intelligent, interesting and your chicken salad tastes like the featured dish at a five-star restaurant."

Iris gave him a dubious look. "You had me up until the part about my chicken salad. That was over-the-top."

"Then maybe it's more about the woman who made the salad than the food itself." Tyler slowly closed the distance between them.

That quickly, the mood in the room changed. It went from stilted and awkward to basic and undeniable. Tyler answered his instincts.

"I don't think this is a good idea." Iris's

words were barely audible.

"Neither do I." But Tyler closed the gap between them and lowered his head to hers.

Iris parted her lips in a silent gasp. Tyler's tongue swept in. His taste was warm, spicy and maybe a little bit wicked, like a half-remembered dream from the deepest part of the night. His touch was bold in a way she hadn't imagined he could be. Her body trembled against him as though her muscles were overwhelmed by the torrent of feelings inside her: surprise, confusion. Desire.

Tyler wrapped his arms around her and pulled her closer. He was big, lean and hard against her. His was definitely not the body of a stereotypical desk jockey. From the way he wore his clothes, she'd suspected he kept fit. Now, up close and personal, she could confirm her suspicions.

Iris wanted to feel this body. To explore it all over. To learn its secrets and share her own. She wrapped her arms around his dome-baby shoulders, rose on her bare toes and pressed herself against him. Heaven.

Tyler growled deep in his throat. The sound was the sexiest thing Iris had ever heard. She shivered against him again. Tyler drew his mouth from hers. He nibbled and kissed his way across her cheek, over her jawline and down her neck. Iris felt cherished by his soft feathered caresses. Her breath shortened. Her pulse raced as her senses came alive. She bent her head back, offering him more of her skin. She wanted these feelings to last. His large, strong hands stroked her back and cupped her waist. How could his touch soothe and excite her at the same time? The man was a mystery.

He slipped his hands past the hem of her garnet jersey, his palms hot against her bare skin. Iris gasped, digging her fingertips into his muscled shoulders. She wanted to touch him. She needed to feel him against her. But when he captured her lace-covered breast, they both froze.

Tyler lifted his head from her neck. His eyes burned with a need, a demand and a question. Iris responded to all three with the smallest movement of her head. A barely noticeable shake that she managed with her last thread of sanity. Tyler released her.

"You're my client." Her words shook. Her throat was dry. Iris willed her arms to drop from his broad shoulders. *Have I ever made a tougher decision?* She couldn't recall.

"You're right." Tyler stepped back. His voice was rough, graveled. "I'm sorry."

"So am I." Iris paced farther into the dining room, giving Tyler plenty of space. She

155

sensed his struggle to hold his desire in check. It was no easy feat for her, either. Her thighs ached with the need for his heat. But he was off-limits.

"I'd better go." Tyler's footsteps sounded across the hardwood flooring behind her.

Iris followed him. "I'll get your coat."

"Thank you again for dinner." Tyler waited while she pulled his coat from the closet.

"You're welcome." The best way to a man's . . . Iris cut off the thought. It wasn't productive. "Good luck with your presentation. I'm sure the executive team will love it."

"They're a tough crowd." Tyler managed a smile though she could still see the heat in his eyes.

"You're not that easy to please, either. If you like it, I'm sure they will, too."

"I hope so." He hesitated a moment or two longer.

Iris waited for him to say whatever else was on his mind. Instead he pivoted toward the door. In one fluid motion he opened it and walked out.

"Good night, Iris." He tossed out the words as though they were an afterthought.

"Good night," she responded to his back.

Iris locked her door, then wandered back to her kitchen. Her mind wove a rich fantasy. What if she and Tyler had met some other way? How would they have spent the weekend? Iris grew warm with the possibilities. Based on her body's reaction to Tyler's kisses, it would have been a weekend to remember. She shook her head as she packed her dishwasher. She'd been open to love — and the joke was on her. Love seemed to have shown itself at the worst possible time. But when "Osiris's Journey" released July 10, her contract with Anderson Adventures would be fulfilled. That was nine weeks from today. They could wait until then, couldn't they?

CHAPTER 8

"They're more interested in the free food than your speech." Donovan pounded Tyler's shoulder.

"That's not helpful." Tyler winced.

Three weeks later, Donovan and Xavier claimed to be keeping Tyler company backstage during the internal game launch. Tyler tugged at his tie in an effort to ease the choke hold at his neck. Was he the only one who felt as though the past four weeks had sped by? He was tense with nerves as the minutes counted down to his presentation. Tyler was tempted to tell Xavier and Donovan to rejoin the associates on the ballroom floor. Neither vice president was scheduled to speak. They were only with him to lend moral support. However, their brand of moral support was making him more anxious.

Foster already had made his remarks, which had officially started the launch more than an hour earlier. He'd then invited everyone to enjoy their lunch. Now the associates were finished with their meal. The servers were clearing the dishes in preparation for Tyler's presentation and the conclusion of the event. The disc jockey they'd hired was still mixing tunes.

Tyler sneaked a glance through the curtains again to observe the crowd. Several associates were chair dancing to the music pumping through the speakers. What if they hated his speech? What if they booed him off the stage or asked the DJ to turn up the music? Even worse, what if they didn't respond at all? So much depended on the event's success.

Where is Iris? He'd insisted on picking her up at her home and driving her to the convention center this morning. But he hadn't seen her since the event started. She'd checked on the audiovisual equipment for the presentations, then followed up with the catering staff, then . . . she was gone, off somewhere else. Was she avoiding him?

He let the curtain drop. It had been almost a month since the night he'd shown up at her place unannounced and uninvited to ask for her help with his speech.

Almost a month since their kiss. But when

he thought about it, he could still taste her, still feel her. That's why he tried hard not to think about it. He needed to try harder.

"You'll be fine." Xavier squeezed his shoulder. It was the same one Donovan had just pounded. "Just stick to your script."

At his cousin's comment, Tyler suddenly couldn't remember a single word of his speech. *Dear God, where is Iris?*

"Are you ready, son?"

Tyler turned to find his father walking toward him.

Aunt Kayla was at Foster's side. "You'll be fine."

Tyler pulled the script from his pocket. He needed to practice it one more time. A hand reached from behind him and took the papers away.

"You already know this." Iris held the script in her hand. "Besides this presentation isn't about reciting words."

"I —" Tyler reached for his speech but she secured the document in her purse.

"And when did you start wearing ties?" She started to reach for him, then dropped her hands. "Please take it off. You need to look approachable."

Tyler removed his tie but his attention remained on his speech in Iris's purse.

Iris addressed Foster. "Are you ready to

introduce our next speaker?"

Foster rubbed his palms together. "Yes, I am. Let's keep the show moving."

"Iris, I need my speech." Tyler's whisper was urgent.

"No, you don't." Iris's hand rested gently on the shoulder Donovan and Xavier had abused. "The thoughts and ideas in the speech aren't new to you. Just remember that this is personal, for you and for them."

Tyler found a measure of calm in her words and her touch. He listened to Foster's introduction as he prepared to take the stage.

"Did you enjoy your lunch?" Foster's question carried through the curtain to Tyler at the back of the stage. The associates responded with thunderous applause.

"Wonderful!" Foster's voice rose above the cacophony. "Good food and good company are important parts of a celebration. And here to tell you just why this particular celebration is so important is my son and your vice president of development, Ty Anderson."

Tyler looked again at Iris. Her coffee-colored eyes shone with supreme confidence. He squared his shoulders, then drew back the curtains to take the stage.

Foster pulled him into a bear hug. "Good

luck, son."

Tyler returned his father's embrace before stepping back to face the roomful of associates. "You're probably a little tired after that wonderful lunch. But don't fall asleep on me yet."

He froze. That's not the way his speech began. Surprised laughter filled the room at his comment. Tyler relaxed a bit.

"I wanted to share a few words with you." Did he sound as awkward as he felt? He kept going. "My father often — or always — says that Anderson Adventures wouldn't be where it is today without all of you. But it recently came to my attention that many of you don't realize how you contribute to our success. So I wanted to take this time to tell you exactly the role you play and to thank you for everything you do. Let's start with purchasing. Will the associates of our purchasing department please stand?" He waited for the four-member staff, including Trudy, the three-time grandmother, to rise from their seats. "Thank you for purchasing the supplies we need to function, the software, hardware and everything else, and for negotiating the very best prices."

The audience gave the department an enthusiastic round of applause. The four purchasing associates stared at each other in surprise. Broad grins brightened their faces and pleased blushes darkened their skin. They each waved at their coworkers before resuming their seats.

Tyler continued in this manner until he'd recognized every department and their responsibilities, and connected them back to the company's success. The pride and satisfaction on the faces around the room were gratifying although it still surprised him that they hadn't realized how important they all were.

What shocked him even more was the standing ovation he received at the end of his presentation. He gazed at the faces in front of him — some admittedly more familiar than others — and finally understood what his father had been saying for years. Anderson Adventures associates weren't employees. They were family.

Foster joined him on stage, wrapping him in another bear hug before stepping back and joining in the applause. Once the noise had died down and their associates had returned to their seats, Tyler provided a brief demonstration of the game, then opened the floor to questions. Excitement filled the room. There was a hum of anticipation. The event was without a doubt the greatest triumph he'd had to date, greater than his award-winning, bestselling computer games.

When it was over much later, Tyler waited in the ballroom with Foster, Aunt Kayla, Iris, Xavier and Donovan to thank their employees once again before they climbed into the limos that would take them back to Anderson Adventures.

"You were right about the limos." Foster turned to him. "Paying for parking after an event like this would have been a buzzkill, as the kids say."

"Ty, I am so proud of you." Aunt Kayla pulled him down so she could kiss his cheek again. "You were wonderful!"

"Thank you, Aunt Kayla." Tyler glanced at Iris. She hadn't said a word since the launch ended. Had he disappointed her?

"You were channeling your inner Steve Harvey." Donovan referenced the popular game-show host.

Xavier grinned. "I knew you had it in you."

"I've never seen you like that before." Foster slapped his back. "You were fantastic. Now take that energy on the road, son."

"What did you think?" Tyler turned to Iris. He couldn't wait any longer. He'd heard from everyone else. Had he lived up to her expectations or not?

"You were perfect. But I knew you would be." Iris's smile mesmerized him.

"Thanks." Tyler wished they were alone so he could kiss her again.

"Your father's right." Iris inclined her head toward Foster. "We need to ride this wave into our external launch and the industry convention next month."

"All right." Tyler couldn't think about the convention. Iris had called him perfect. "Are you ready to leave?"

Iris checked her silver Omni wristwatch. "Are we going into the office?"

"I wasn't planning to."

She adjusted the shoulder strap of her briefcase. "I was going to get some work done."

"I insist you take the rest of the afternoon off." Foster looked at Xavier, Donovan and Tyler. "In fact, everyone go home. Our associates have the afternoon off. The rest of us should, too."

Donovan turned to Xavier. "Let's go before he changes his mind."

"I'm waiting for you." Xavier pulled his car keys from his pocket as he led the way to the parking garage.

Foster offered Kayla his arm. "I'll take you home."

Kayla cocked her head. "I hope so since

you drove me here."

Tyler turned to Iris. "That leaves us. Should I take you to the office?"

Iris shook her head. "I can work from home."

"Then I'll take you home." Tyler adjusted his stride to hers as they left the center's ballroom.

He wanted to offer her his arm the way his father had offered his arm to Kayla. But he'd been on shaky ground with her since the night she'd helped him with his speech. He watched her in his peripheral vision. Did she ever recall that night? Probably not. The realization bothered him. While she seemed unaffected by their intimacy, his palm still burned with the phantom feel of soft lace and warm woman.

Minutes later, Iris watched Tyler pay the parking attendant before merging his silver Honda Accord with the rest of the traffic on Front Street. When he'd picked her up from her town house that morning, Tyler had been anxious and preoccupied. Now that the launch had been a success, she'd expected the atmosphere in the four-door sedan to be more relaxed. Instead, Tyler seemed to be brooding. Was he worried about the external launch?

Iris waited until Tyler had pulled up to a red traffic light. "We'll send the wrap-up email Monday morning, then turn our complete attention to the external campaign."

If anything, Tyler's expression became grimmer. "I still don't think I'm the right person to do the media interviews or attend the industry conference."

"Foster's convinced you are." Iris's left palm itched to cup his strong jaw. The memory of his mouth moving on her skin made her body burn. She tore her eyes from his profile and stared through the windshield. "We have a late flight to San Diego for the electronic games conference in June."

"I'll drive us to the airport and leave my car in the lot." The light turned green. Tyler eased into the intersection.

"Thank you." Iris watched pedestrians hurrying down Broad Street. Their hands were buried deep in their coats and their bodies were bent against the wind. It was late afternoon in early May but the air still had a bite.

Although Foster had insisted they take the rest of the afternoon off, Iris spent their commute discussing media interviews and goals for the industry conference. Tyler's contributions consisted of short answers and toneless *hmm*s. Thirty minutes later, Tyler pulled onto her driveway and parked in front of her garage. He turned off the engine and released his seat belt.

"Thank you for driving me home." Iris looked at him warily. This morning, he'd circled his sedan to hold the passenger door for her. This afternoon, he just sat there.

"You're welcome."

"Congratulations again on the successful internal launch." Iris unbuckled her seat belt, preparing to climb from his car. "I'll see you Monday."

"It's been a month." Tyler's ebony eyes held her in place. "Do you ever even think about it?"

Her lips parted. "The kiss?"

Tyler's gaze lowered briefly to her breasts before returning to her eyes. "It was more than a kiss."

An electric current arced between them. She couldn't be the only one who felt it. It was a very different type of tension from the one that had plagued them that morning.

"Yes, I've thought about it." *I've thought about that night and the way you made me feel more than I should.*

"Right now, I really wish I wasn't your client." Tyler glared at her garage door through the windshield.

"But you are."

"Why does that mean that I can't touch you? Or taste you?"

Iris fought the sensual assault of his words. "I don't have personal relationships with clients."

Tyler gave her a heated look. "Is that all I am to you, a client?"

Iris arched an eyebrow. "Am I more than a vendor to you?"

Tyler captured her left hand and held it to his chest under his jacket and above his heart. "A vendor's never made me feel like this."

Against her palm, Iris felt his heartbeat. It was racing, just like hers. She searched his hot ebony eyes. She wanted to give in to him. "We can't. We both have too much at stake to take that risk."

Still holding her palm to his chest, Tyler closed his eyes. "It's going to be a long nine weeks."

Iris smiled. He was right. "Don't think about that. Focus on your success, including Foster admitting he was wrong about the limo service."

Tyler opened his eyes. "Dad's good about admitting when someone else has a good idea. He's also good at reminding us when he's been right. I'm sure he'll remind me that contacting you had been his idea."

"Foster told you to ask me to bid on this project?" Iris had a sense of foreboding.

"But it was my decision which vendor to retain."

"How did he hear about my company?" Iris slipped free of Tyler's hold and leaned back on the passenger's car seat. Something felt off. *What am I missing?*

"I don't know." Tyler shrugged. "He said he knew your family but I didn't ask how."

"I think I know." Iris gritted her teeth. *Rose.*

Iris parked on Rose's driveway and slammed out of her car Friday evening. She marched up the front steps of her sister's two-story white-and-black home, then leaned on the doorbell. Rose yanked open her door. She was still wearing her business clothes, a smoke-gray skirt suit and a bloodred blouse.

"What is wrong with you?" Her sister's choice of words was like gasoline on a fire.

"You are." Iris was six years old again as she stormed the threshold, forcing Rose back into her house.

Rose shoved Iris aside and slammed her front door shut. "Do you want to tell me why you've brought your temper tantrum into my home?"

Iris turned to face her. Her hands were fisted at her sides. "You told Foster Anderson to hire me."

"Who?" Rose settled her hands on her hips.

"Don't play dumb." Iris slashed her right hand in the air. "You know Foster Anderson owns Anderson Adventures."

Rose's confusion cleared. "Ah. I've heard the name. I don't know the man."

"You know him well enough to tell him to give me a job." Iris's voice rose.

"No, I don't. I've never spoken with him."

"You're lying."

"Are you nuts?" Rose's eyes widened.

"You don't believe I can get business on my own. So instead, you used your connections to convince Anderson Adventures to throw some work my way."

"I thought you said this was a big account." Rose tilted her head.

"It is."

"Then they did more than just throw some work your way."

"Are you proud of what you've done?" Iris narrowed her eyes. "I don't need your pity efforts. I'm good enough to get my own work."

"What makes you think I know Foster Anderson personally?"

Iris took a deep breath, trying to control her temper. "Tyler told me his father knows our family."

"I repeat." Rose crossed her arms and gave Iris a cool stare. "What makes you think I know him?"

"You're the one who doesn't believe I can succeed." Iris glared at Rose. "Who else would go begging for work for me?"

"I would." Lily's voice came from behind her.

Iris spun in the direction of Rose's living room. She stared at her middle sister in surprise. "I thought you believed in me."

"I do." Lily stood in the threshold between Rose's living room and the front entrance. "That's why I gave Foster Anderson your business card and asked him to keep you in mind if his company needed a marketing consultant."

"I can get clients on my own." Never in a million years would Iris have imagined Lily would betray her.

All of her life, Lily had been there for her with words of encouragement. She'd supported Iris's dream of working for a public relations firm in New York straight out of college when everyone else thought a smaller market like Columbus was a safer plan. Lily had also agreed with her decision to leave a good job in New York and return to Columbus when Iris had gotten homesick. And when Iris had quit her well-paying job seven months ago, Lily had defended Iris's goal of opening her own marketing and public relations firm when Rose had told Iris to get a job with a pension plan.

Lily stepped forward. "Iris, you were furious when that young man at your previous job used his connections to get the promotion you'd been working toward. But networking is how you get ahead in business."

"Lil's right." Rose moved to stand beside Lily. "It's not what you know. It's who you know. You should have learned that lesson well from your last job."

"But I don't want to get ahead that way." Iris sighed with frustration. "I want to build my reputation on my abilities."

"Don't be naive, Pollyanna." Rose grunted. "Take off the pink shades and see the world the way it is."

"That's not helpful, Rose." Lily turned back to Iris. "You've proven you can do both. *I* didn't get you the Anderson Adventures account. All I did was give

Foster Anderson your name. You did the work."

Iris sighed. "I wish you'd told me what you were doing."

"You'd have tried to talk her out of it." Rose tilted her head. "It seems to me based on your reaction to what Lily did, *you're* the one who doesn't have confidence in your abilities, not us."

Iris gaped at Rose. "That's not true."

Rose crossed her arms. "Then why are you so upset that Lily gave you a reference? You don't have to do everything yourself."

Maybe Rose and Lily were right. She was making a scene because of her own insecurities. After all, Lily did what she'd always done: supported Iris's dreams.

"I'm sorry." Iris reached out and took Lily's hand. "I appreciate what you did."

Lily shook her head. "I was only trying to help, Iris."

"I know." Iris sighed. Self-doubt was a vicious thing and a lot harder to conquer than she would've thought. "I want to prove that I can succeed with my own agency. But Rosie's right. I don't have to do it all myself. I shouldn't have reacted so poorly."

"Don't worry about it. No hard feelings." Lily smiled, giving Iris a quick hug before stepping back. "And I have complete faith in you, Iris. You should know that by now. Your agency will be a great success. You'll see." Lily glanced at Rose. "You'll both see. And then I'll say, 'I told you so.' "

CHAPTER 9

At Anderson Adventures Thursday morning, a little more than two weeks before the industry convention, Iris turned the corner on her way back to her office. She came to an abrupt stop. Lauren appeared to be waiting for her outside the locked room.

Several company associates had given Iris their opinion of Xavier's girlfriend of four months. They agreed she was beautiful. Tall and slender, Lauren wore her professional polish with an ease Iris struggled for every day. But no one seemed to like the woman, including Xavier's mother.

"There you are." Lauren greeted her with a cool smile. Her sleek cap of dark brown hair framed her thin face.

"Are you waiting for me?" Iris couldn't think of a single reason why.

"I heard the internal launch went well." Lauren's ice-blue linen skirt suit fit her as though custom-made. Her matching sapphire jewelry — earrings, necklace and bracelets — looked expensive.

"Yes, it did." The event had occurred almost two weeks ago. Why was Lauren bringing it up now?

"Ty must be pleased." Lauren stepped away from Iris's locked office door and faced her.

"We all are." The energy and excitement the launch had generated still pulsed throughout the company. They were feeding Tyler's confidence, as well as her own.

"I'm sorry I wasn't able to attend." Lauren settled her hands on her slim hips. "But Ty insisted the launch was for employees only."

"Associates, and yes, it was." She still wasn't clear on the reason Lauren had sought her out, but she had the feeling it wasn't to congratulate her.

"Was that your decision?"

Was she kidding? "I'm an outside consultant. I don't make decisions for the company." Why was Lauren questioning *her* about the launch? Shouldn't she be speaking with Xavier or Tyler?

"Then it was Ty's decision." Lauren drummed her well-manicured fingertips on her hip bones. Her nails were coated with black polish.

"The executive team approved it. That includes Foster, Kayla, Xavier, Van and, yes, Ty."

"I know who the executives are, sweetie." Lauren's smile didn't make it to her brown eyes.

"Of course you do." Iris glanced around the hallway. She wasn't comfortable having this conversation with Lauren out in the open. But to escort the other woman into her office would imply she was encouraging Lauren's confidences.

She wasn't.

Lauren continued. "I understand that the external launch starts in two weeks."

"You know a lot about the project launches."

Lauren gave her a cat-who-ate-the-canary smile. "Xavier confides in me."

"Then I can't tell you anything you don't already know." Iris circled Xavier's girlfriend to get to her office. As she drew closer, she caught the scent of Lauren's perfume. Like its wearer, it lacked subtlety.

"Actually, there's something you can tell me." Lauren's voice followed Iris.

"What is it?" With great reluctance, Iris faced Lauren again.

"Will the conference be a success?"

I hope so. "Everything is ready. We have

our media talking points, presentations and demonstrations."

"You didn't answer my question." Lauren gave Iris a cool smile. "Will the conference be a success?"

"Yes, it will." Iris sent up a prayer.

"Which means Ty will get his way and become the next CEO of Anderson Adventures." Lauren's voice dripped with disgust.

"My focus is on launching the game successfully. I'm not concerned with who runs the company."

"I am." Lauren dropped her hands from her hips. "Ty was groomed to ascend to the throne but Xavier would be a much better leader for the company."

Why was Lauren involving her in this discussion? "Neither of us is in a position to weigh in on that decision."

"Do you believe Ty's ready to lead Anderson Adventures?" Lauren's dark eyes pinned her.

"Lauren, I don't know what you're after but I don't want any part of it." With that, Iris swiped her security badge through the reader on the conference room door and escaped into her office. The door locked behind her, leaving Lauren in the hallway.

What was that about?

Iris crossed to the glass table and sat in front of her laptop. She tapped the space bar to reawaken her computer. The monitor returned to her Microsoft Outlook screen.

Darn it! I forgot to lock my computer. Again.

Tyler had made her promise to follow their security procedures. Well, at least she'd remembered to close the office's security door when she'd gone to the restroom. But now that she thought about it, she didn't remember using her email before she'd left the room.

Two weeks later, Tyler rode a crowded elevator with Iris in the host hotel of the Electronic Gaming Convention in San Diego. Iris's citrus-and-vanilla scent surrounded him. He was spending four days in a fancy hotel with a beautiful woman he couldn't touch, doing his least favorite thing: promotion. Fate could be cruel.

The elevator opened on the sixth floor. Several passengers disembarked, including Iris. Tyler followed her.

"Your suite's on the twelfth floor." She hesitated, seeming surprised to find him with her.

"I know." Tyler scanned the hallway for the signs that would direct them to Iris's room. "I'm going to escort you to your room."

"You don't need to do that."

"Yes, I do." It was more than manners. He felt protective of her.

"All right. But good luck getting an elevator to your floor." Iris pulled her wheeled suitcase behind her. "They're all going to be as crowded as the one we just left."

Tyler followed her, pulling his own suitcase. "I don't understand why you booked me on a separate floor. I would've been fine in one of these rooms."

"You need a suite. Or would you be comfortable with reporters sitting on your bed while they interview you?"

Tyler shrugged. "I guess it would depend on the reporter."

"A little adolescent flashback?" Iris shook her head with a smile. "After we unpack, we'll review your schedule and talking points for tomorrow's presentation."

Tyler glanced at his Movado wristwatch. It was six o'clock in the evening in San Diego, nine o'clock at night back home in Columbus. He was starving.

"I know you're in charge but I'd rather eat first." Tyler stopped in front of Iris's room.

"All right. We can order room service and

make it a working dinner." She swiped her key card through the reader on her hotel door.

"Oh, joy."

Still smiling, she gave him a sarcastic look over her shoulder. "Let's look at a menu."

Tyler followed Iris into her room. He stood his luggage against the wall beside the door. His black loafers sank into thick blue-gray carpeting as he followed her into her room. The narrow entrance was framed by a closet with mirrored sliding doors on the left and a bathroom on the right. Beyond the entryway, a black flat-screen television stood on a cherrywood chest of drawers. His attention lingered on the king-size bed.

Iris set her suitcase and carry-on beside the bed. The room-service menu was on the desk near the floral-patterned armchair. She gave it a quick read through, then handed it to Tyler. "I'll take the chicken sandwich and fries, and a bottle of water."

Tyler skimmed the choices, then gave her back the menu. "Me, too. I'll place the orders. We'll eat in my room."

More than two hours later, Tyler's brain threatened to explode. He and Iris had eaten dinner in his suite's small sitting area. He'd taken the armchair, leaving the sofa to her. It was an awkward setup made even more uncomfortable by her interrogation. Between bites of her french fries and chicken sandwich loaded with everything but onions, Iris had quizzed him on their schedule for the convention's media day, and his talking points for the press, as well as the gamers. She'd impersonated an avid fan so well, he'd forgotten she'd never played a computer game in her life. But her performance as an investigative journalist made him want to evict her from his room.

"I still don't understand why *I'm* here instead of Van." Though the image of Donovan and Iris in an intimate hotel room put him in danger of losing his dinner.

"You've been asking that question for months. The answer hasn't changed." Iris's voice was rich with unwelcomed humor. "Besides, as vice president for product development, don't you want to meet the people who enjoy your games?"

Tyler stood, stacking their used dishes onto the room-service tray. "You're right. It will be helpful to get their feedback firsthand."

"You're agreeing with me?" Iris's eyes widened. "Wait, I need to mark this date on my calendar."

"And the award for Best Performance in a Drama goes to Iris Beharie." Tyler placed the tray in the hallway, then returned to Iris. "Are you done?"

"I'd like to thank the Academy . . ."

Tyler struggled against a smile as he sat. "Are the reporters going to be as confrontational as you were during our run-through?"

"They'll be worse." Iris slid her notes back into her project folder. "But don't worry. You handled this practice session like a pro."

"I should probably be more nervous this time around." Tyler gave a mental shrug. "This is a larger audience than our associates' launch. And they won't be as forgiving. But for some reason, I'm more at ease this time. Maybe it'll hit me tomorrow."

Iris crossed her long legs. Her vivid green skirt suit added a glow to her honey skin. After their long day of travel from Columbus to San Diego, she should be wrinkled and tired. Instead, she looked like a fashion model on a photo shoot for a line of power suits.

There were so many sides to Iris Beharie. The consummate professional who'd presented her product launch proposal during their first meeting. The fighter who'd defended herself when he'd confronted her over what turned out to be false rumors of unethical behavior. The siren with whom he'd almost lost control the evening he'd asked for her help with his presentation. Who would she reveal next?

"Maybe you're more relaxed this time because the internal launch was more important to you." Iris's shrug seemed restless. "Anderson Adventures is like a family. We're more concerned about our family's reaction than what strangers think."

What had he heard in her voice? Tension? Uncertainty? "How did your family feel about your quitting your job?"

Iris lowered her gaze. "Lily, my middle sister, was supportive. But Rose, the oldest, thought I'd lost my mind. I think she would've had me committed for psychological evaluation if it weren't for Lily."

Tyler was torn between laughter and outrage on her behalf. "How does Rose feel about your venture now?"

"She's still worried." Iris gave him a rueful smile. "Success is the only thing that will prove to Rose that I can be successful."

"She sounds like my father." Tyler's eyes roamed over Iris's elegant features. He could spend the rest of the night looking at her.

"I wish she'd give me credit for knowing what I'm doing." Iris's right calf began to swing in a now familiar gesture. "I sound like a sulky adolescent, seeking my older sister's approval."

"I feel the same way about my father." Tyler leaned forward, resting his forearms on his knees. "But I think he and your sister will change their minds once this launch is over."

"You're right." Iris gave him her special smile. "We make a good team."

"Yes, we do." The realization filled him with excitement for his future.

Anderson Adventures was releasing "Osiris's Journey" in a little more than five weeks. Tyler's body tightened with anticipation. The release would signal the end of Iris's professional commitment to his company. Then they'd be free to pursue a personal relationship.

He considered Iris. Is that what she wanted, too? He prayed that she did. He couldn't imagine himself returning to a life without Iris Beharie.

"Exciting craftsmanship."

"Gorgeous graphics."

" 'Osiris's Journey' is a truly skillful game that fans will obsess over."

Iris wanted to pump her fist in the air. She continued to eavesdrop on gamers and reporters after Tyler's presentation Thursday afternoon. Media day. She'd been posting photos and messages on Twitter, Facebook, Instagram and Pinterest since they'd arrived at the convention. She sent a tweet with the overheard comments as she wound her way through the audience to the back of the hotel ballroom's makeshift stage. The area was thick with reporters from every type of news outlet: industry publications, local newspapers, international journals, radio, television and e-zines. Tyler had impressed them all with his presentation. She finally caught up with him backstage.

"You were wonderful." Without thinking, she gave him a congratulatory hug. She caught her breath when he pulled her even tighter to his long, hard body.

"All thanks to you."

"You're giving me too much credit." Reluctantly, Iris stepped back. It was cold outside of his embrace. "You didn't seem nervous at all."

"Why would I be nervous when my lucky charm was with me?"

"What lucky charm?" In the three months they'd been working together, he'd never mentioned one before.

"You."

The look in his ebony eyes made her body burn.

A couple of times during his presentation, Tyler's gaze had found hers in the crowded ballroom. She'd given him a smile and received one of his slow, sexy grins in return. Was that the reason he'd sought her in the audience, because he thought she brought him good luck? She was flattered. The idea warmed her, made her want to throw her arms around him again. Tempting, but it wouldn't be a good idea.

Before she gave into her desires, Iris pivoted on her heel to lead Tyler into the hotel's hallway. The bright white walls and strong lighting were in dramatic contrast to the more intimate shadows backstage. The chill of the air-conditioning felt good on her flushed cheeks.

"You were a natural on stage. I could have heard a pin drop during your presentation." *Am I babbling?*

"Let's get some dinner." Tyler laid his large palm on the small of her back to guide her toward the hotel's front doors.

"We should get ready for your interview with the reporter from *The Gamer's Seat.*" Iris struggled to keep Tyler focused on the convention. It was hard enough keeping herself on task when she could feel the heat of his touch through her deep gold suit jacket.

Tyler continued toward the hotel's entrance. "That's not until tomorrow afternoon. We have plenty of time."

"Why don't we just eat in the hotel?" Iris pointed behind her toward the busy restaurant that was fast disappearing from view as Tyler moved her relentlessly through the lobby.

"Iris, we're in San Diego." Tyler escorted her through the glass-and-metal doors. "We're not spending the entire convention in the hotel. Let's try to enjoy at least part of our time here."

Iris blinked at him. Since when had Tyler Anderson, an admitted workaholic, wanted to enjoy himself? "I thought your idea of enjoyment was spending long hours at your desk."

Tyler gave her a sarcastic look. "I'm taking a page from your book and learning to enjoy my surroundings."

Iris had a hard time remaining immune to an uptight Tyler Anderson. Did she have the fortitude to resist his more fun-loving, even sexier persona? Did she want to?

Almost three hours later, Tyler escorted Iris to her hotel room. He'd capped his media day success with a great Mexican dinner and the company of a charming and intelligent woman. He didn't want to end the evening.

"Thank you again for dinner." Iris dug her room card key from her handbag before looking up at him. "It was the perfect way to celebrate your triumph."

Tyler matched his footsteps to Iris's as he walked beside her down the hotel's hallways. "It wouldn't have been a success without you. I feel like the high scorer in a quest game."

She gave him the smile that punched him in the gut, taking his breath away. "Are you finally glad you're here instead of Van?"

Tyler was lost in her warm, coffee eyes; tempted by her full, red lips; intoxicated by her cool feminine scent. "I suppose I am."

"Even though you have another interview tomorrow afternoon?" Iris stopped in front of her room. She unlocked her door, then pushed it open.

"I'm looking forward to it."

"Who are you and what have you done with Ty Anderson?" Iris's low laughter caused the muscle beneath Tyler's belt to stir.

Tyler let the door close behind them and scanned her room. It looked uninhabited. Where were her personal items? He wanted to see the perfume she wore. What brand of lipstick gave her lips that moist, kissable look? Where was the lotion that made her skin so soft? The only items in plain sight were her laptop and project folders.

Iris crossed to the desk. "I was going to review this with you after the press conference this afternoon."

"I'm glad we went to dinner instead." Tyler tracked her progress across the room — long, graceful strides in her three-inch heels. Her dark gold shoes were an almost perfect match to her skirt suit.

"So am I." She passed him the top folder.

Tyler took it from her and grasped her hand. "I meant what I said. The success we're having at this convention is all due to you."

Iris blushed. "You have a talent for promoting Anderson Adventures' games. Don't discount it."

"You bring out the best in me."

"That's one of the nicest things anyone's ever said to me."

Tyler stepped closer. "You've helped me come out of my shell. With your help, I've done things I never thought I'd be able to do, like the launch presentation to our associates and media day."

Iris's dark eyes held his. "But you've always had the ability in you." She tapped her slender palm against his chest twice. "Right here."

Tyler captured her hand, holding it in place.

She didn't pull away.

Before he could reconsider his next move, he made it.

Chapter 10

She tasted so good. Tyler wanted to drink from her lips forever. So sweet. Intoxicating. Iris's lips were soft and supple beneath his, exploring him just as he explored her. He traced his tongue along the seam of her lips. Iris opened for him. The muscles tensed in his gut. Tyler sighed into her mouth. He stroked her tongue. Iris suckled his in turn, teasing him, playing with him in a manner that brought to mind another area of his anatomy.

He released her hand, which he'd held to his chest, and wrapped his arms around her warmth and softness. Iris moved against him as though she couldn't stay still. Tyler's pulse beat a hard, fast rhythm that echoed in his ears.

But what if she wanted him to stop again?

Tyler lifted his head, breaking their kiss. "Is this what you want?" Rough and deep, he didn't recognize his own voice.

"Yes, *you're* what I want." Iris's eyes were soft as they searched his.

"Are you sure?" It was killing him to ask. But it would hurt even worse to leave her again.

"Positive." Iris rose up on her toes, lifting her hands to his shoulders, and kissed him.

This time her kiss was rough, demanding. Tyler held her closer, reveling in her assertiveness. She kissed him, over and over again. She explored his mouth and let him explore the way his body wanted to move against hers. She was beautiful, sexy and smart. His wicked fantasy come to warm, wonderful life in his arms.

Tyler released her to unbutton her suit jacket. He parted the garment and stepped back. His hungry eyes feasted on her firm, perfect breasts in a black lace bra. Tyler swallowed a groan. He reached out to touch her bare skin. Her abdominal muscles trembled beneath his fingertips. Iris moaned and reached for him, kissing him again. She sighed into his mouth as her hands tugged at his clothes. Tyler lifted his head and stepped back to help her. He pulled his wallet from the back pocket of his slacks and tossed it onto the mattress for easy access later.

Within minutes, their clothes were off and

they stood before each other. The look in Iris's dark eyes as they moved over his chest, hips and thighs caused Tyler's erection to swell even more. She ran her fingers down his torso with the lightest touch. Tyler's muscles shook.

Iris lifted her wide eyes to his. "Your body is amazing."

"You're so beautiful." Tyler's gaze moved over her firm breasts, tight waist and slim, well-rounded hips.

Tyler reached for her breast, testing its weight in the palm of his hand. Her nipple grew with his attention. He wrapped an arm around her waist and lifted her as he lowered his head to her chest. He took her breast into his mouth. Iris's gasps and moans urged him on. He laved her nipple, circling the hardened tip with his tongue, stroking it as it pebbled in his mouth.

Iris's body shook in his embrace. Tyler walked her backward to the bed. He lifted her into his arms and lowered her onto the mattress.

Iris rose up on her knees. "Come to me."

"I'm right here." Tyler joined her on the mattress. He reached for her but Iris surprised him, pressing him onto the bed.

She straddled him, then lowered her lips to his, kissing him hard and deep as her hands roamed his chest, rubbed his nipples and stroked his torso. Her kisses traveled from his mouth to his jawline and down his neck.

"I love the way you smell," she whispered against his ear.

"You smell like heaven." Tyler ran the back of his hands over the soft skin of her breasts. "And feel like my fantasies."

Iris lifted her head to look down at him. A smile hovered around her lips. "You've been fantasizing about me?"

Tyler grinned without apology. "If you only knew."

"I've had a few fantasies of my own."

Tyler's smile vanished. She'd actually rendered him speechless.

Iris tossed him a heated look before moving down his body. She paused to caress his nipples with her lips and tongue. Tyler's blood began to heat. His stomach muscles danced beneath her touch. His body stiffened. Iris stopped just above his hips. She blew a soft breath against his length. Tyler gritted his teeth. Her tongue slid up his length from his tip to his root once, twice.

The third time, she took him into her mouth.

Tyler's hips rose off the bed. He pressed

his head hard into the pillow. Iris worked her hands, lips and tongue on his sensitive skin. She stroked him, kissed him, circled her tongue around him. She moved fast and then slow, pushing him to the edge of his self-control.

He filled his lungs to make his plea. "Stop."

Iris slowly released him. "Did I do something wrong?"

The uncertainty in her voice almost shredded him. "You did everything too right. But I want to come inside you."

She gave him a sexy smile, then lay down beside him.

Tyler pressed her onto her back. "My turn."

Iris trembled with desire as Tyler came to her. He lowered his head to her breasts and drew one into his mouth. Iris bit her lips together to keep from screaming with pleasure. She arched her back to offer him more. His teeth grazed her nipple. His tongue teased and stroked. Iris couldn't catch her breath.

Tyler slid down her body, touching and teasing her, exploring her sensitive spots. He moved between her legs, spreading them wider. Then he rose on his knees, cupped her hips and lifted her to his mouth.

Iris's eyes flared wide. Her mouth opened on a gasp as he stroked his tongue against her. Hard. And kissed her. Deep. She was a puppet in his palms. Her hips moved against his mouth as his tongue and lips directed her. Iris's body flooded with heat. She panted and gasped and groaned under his magic. He loved her with private kisses and long, leisurely licks. Her muscles strained. Her body stretched and tensed. Then she exploded, rocking in his hands. Tyler soothed her with his touch as he lowered her to the mattress.

Iris felt him move away from her. She opened her eyes and watched as he put on a condom. Tyler turned back to her. His ebony eyes moved over her body. Iris's heart raced. Her thighs throbbed.

Tyler caressed the side of her breast. "So beautiful."

He lowered himself to her gently, then joined with her in one long, strong, deep push.

His hips moved, picking up a rhythm that fanned her desires. Iris wrapped her legs around Tyler's hips and met him thrust for thrust. She looked up at his handsome face. His features were hard and sharp with desire. His intense gaze locked with hers as they moved as one. He lowered his head and kissed her hard. His hips moved deeper, faster. Iris's blood rushed through her veins and roared in her head. Her heart pounded as though it would burst from her chest. She lifted her hips higher, pressing harder and harder against him. She squeezed her eyes shut at the sweet pleasure-pain.

Her body shattered, trembling in his embrace. Tyler stiffened above her, drawing her closer as they bodies shook together.

A long time later, Tyler stirred. "I don't regret what we did. I don't want you to, either."

His words disrupted the stillness in the room. Perhaps he'd let the silence last a little too long. It was becoming tense — or was that his imagination? In any event, he meant it when he said he didn't want either of them to have regrets.

"I don't." Iris rested her head on his chest.

Her simple reply brought him a measure of relief. Still, Tyler needed to be sure. He hadn't planned for this to happen, at least not tonight. But he wouldn't change a thing. Would she?

He measured his words. "I know we'd agreed to wait because of our project contract."

"I wouldn't have made love with you if I thought I was going to regret it."

"I'm glad." That's all he'd needed to hear.

Tyler relaxed. He buried his right hand in her thick, tousled hair. His left held her to him. Iris had said they'd "made love." The words expanded in his heart like a sunrise. He breathed in her scent, citrus and sex.

"But what do we do now? Act like nothing happened?" Iris's breath tickled his skin.

"That's not possible." He watched the shadows stretching across the ceiling. What time was it? Did he care?

"No, it's not." Her soft breasts pressed into him with her sigh.

Tyler's muscles tightened with a pleasure that was almost painful. "We're doing that a lot more lately, agreeing with each other.

"That's because you're finally coming to your senses."

"Maybe you're the one who's seeing reason."

"Impossible." Iris waved a dismissive hand, then let it land on his chest. Her tone sobered. "I don't want people to know we've been intimate. I'm your marketing consultant. This could damage my professional reputation."

"That was the reason you didn't want to become intimate in the first place." Tyler pressed her hand against his heart. "I'm not going to announce that we've made love.

But I'm not going to act as though I'm not attracted to you, either."

"All right." She sighed again. "I have another concern."

"What is it?"

Iris folded her arms on his torso to prop herself up. Cool air slipped between them. "You once accused me of using Anderson Adventures as a dating service. I don't want you to think I came on to you for mercenary reasons."

"I don't. I trust you." And he did. Tyler cupped her beautiful face with his left palm. "Besides, I know you want me for my body."

Iris trailed her fingertips from his chest down his torso. "It's a great body — for a gamer."

"That's an unfair and inaccurate generalization of my people." Tyler ignored his quivering stomach muscles.

"Oh, yeah?" She'd lowered her voice to a sexy, taunting whisper. "I've heard gamers tend to be twenty-pound weaklings." Iris gave him an arched look that heated his blood. "I've met a few in my time."

"I think you can see I'm not a twenty-pound weakling." His voice was rough with desire.

Iris covered his body with her own, making his erection throb. "Show me."

201

Tyler rolled, bringing her with him. His quick reflexes surprised a gasp from her lips. He drew her under him and held her gaze with his own. "With pleasure."

He lowered his head and captured her lips.

The next morning, Iris paced Tyler's hotel room. She checked her silver wristwatch again. "The reporter from *The Gamer's Seat* is supposed to be here in ten minutes. I've heard he's usually early, though."

"We'll be ready whenever he arrives." Tyler settled onto a corner of the sofa.

Iris stopped to study him. In his black polo shirt and steel-gray slacks, he made an incongruous image against the pink-and-red floral-patterned sofa. But the dark clothing made him look dangerously sexy. Her stomach muscles quivered every time she remembered the way he'd touched her through the night. Iris shook her head to clear the image from her mind.

"Maybe we should look at one of the other articles he's written." She began pacing again.

Had she done everything she could to prepare her client for this interview? Had she given every effort to present Tyler in the best possible light to the public?

"We've already dissected three of his most

recent ones." Tyler propped his right ankle on his left knee. "We don't need to look at any more."

"He's going to want to know about the game reveal, its features as a first-person game, its remote-play functionality and platforms —"

"Iris." Tyler's low voice brought her to a sudden halt.

"Yes?"

"Sit down." He gestured toward the armchair beside him. "You've done a great job prepping me. Everything will be fine."

"You're right." Iris took a deep breath as she crossed to the sitting area. She ran her hand down the front of her conservative sapphire dress, then lowered herself onto the armchair. "I'm sorry."

"Our roles have reversed." Tyler tossed her a smile. "Now you're the tense one and I'm calm."

A loud knock sounded on the door. Iris frowned at it. "I told you he'd be early."

Tyler rose from the sofa. "And I told you we'd be ready when he arrived."

Iris stood as Tyler answered the door. Ryan Tipper, the reporter from *The Gamer's Seat,* was even more rumpled than photos of him suggested. He looked as though he hadn't shaved since he'd arrived at the convention. Judging by the dark gold stain on his dull white shirt beneath his mud-brown blazer, he liked spicy mustard.

The reporter shoved his shaggy brown hair back from his glasses. "I'm Ryan Tipper of *The Gamer's Seat.* And you're Ty Anderson. Nice job with your launch yesterday."

"Nice to meet you." Tyler offered his right hand. "Come in."

"Thanks." Ryan paused when Iris stepped forward. He adjusted the satchel on his left shoulder.

"Iris Beharie. I'm Mr. Anderson's marketing consultant." Iris held out her hand. "Thank you for coming."

Ryan looked surprised. "Sure, sure. I appreciate the exclusive." His hand was soft and damp.

"Let's sit." Iris tugged her hand free.

She nodded toward Tyler, indicating he should take the armchair. Iris gestured Ryan to precede her to the sofa.

"Okay, I'll jump right in." Ryan flipped open his satchel and unpacked an audio recorder. He pressed a couple of buttons on the machine then turned toward Tyler. "This is the Tyler Anderson interview. Today is Friday, June fifth. Ty, how are you enjoying 'Osiris's Journey' 's gameplay reveal?"

Iris gave a mental nod. He'd started with

the softball questions just as she'd anticipated based on her research of the reporter's interviewing style. She sat back on the opposite end of the sofa and observed the interview. Tyler did a fantastic job. He was composed, concise and confident. Everything she could have hoped.

" 'Osiris's Journey' will be available on all current platforms simultaneously," Tyler said.

"All on the release date?"

Tyler nodded. "Yes, on July tenth."

Ryan glanced over his shoulder at Iris before he turned back to Tyler. "Will the game be ready in time?"

Tyler looked puzzled. "It's ready now."

"Are you sure?" Ryan glanced briefly at Iris again.

Iris's brows knitted. *Why does he keep looking at me?*

"I'm quite sure." Tyler's frown deepened.

Ryan arched a brow. "But 'Osiris's Journey' has failed its product tests."

Iris blinked her surprise. She sat straighter on the sofa, fisting her hands to keep from interjecting. *Let Ty handle this.*

Surprise cleared the frown from Tyler's sharp sienna features. "Your information is wrong."

Ryan slid another look toward Iris. "I

don't think so."

"You saw the reveal in the presentation." Tyler sat forward.

"We all know there are ways to fake a game's readiness for the press." Ryan looked stubborn.

The claim was too outrageous for Iris to remain silent any longer. "Where did you get your information?"

The shaggy reporter stared at her in surprise. "I'll never reveal my sources." His tone was almost comically sincere.

"Your sources have given you bad information." Tyler bit the words. "With minor enhancements, the game will be ready for release July tenth."

" 'Minor enhancements'?" Ryan chuckled. "You said the game was ready now."

"We could put it on the market today." Tyler spoke with strained patience. "But these enhancements will make the game more robust."

"What evidence do your sources have to prove 'Osiris's Journey' failed its testing?" Iris demanded. "Or are you just taking their word for it?" —

Ryan looked at Iris in confusion. "No, they sent me the test results."

"The hell they did." Tyler sounded as though his head was about to explode.

The reporter dug into his satchel again. "Here. Look."

Tyler scanned the stack of papers Ryan handed him. He looked shocked. Iris rose to look over Tyler's shoulder. Her eyes widened. Her lips parted in shock. How did the reporter get ahold of these documents? The information was printed on Anderson Adventures electronic letter-head. Adding insult to injury, printed across the top in big block red letters was the word *Confidential.*

Tyler lifted his head to look at Ryan. "These tests are dated two months ago. We've had several much more recent tests. They all prove 'Osiris's Journey' is ready for market."

Ryan looked at Iris in confusion. He turned back to Tyler. "So you say."

"I can send you the latest test results." Tyler stood, indicating the interview was over.

"We'll send you those results as soon as we return to the office." Iris straightened from her position behind Tyler. "Until then, I'd advise you against printing even a hint that 'Osiris's Journey' isn't market ready."

"But —" Ryan looked up at her.

"Such a claim would be knowingly false," Iris continued. "I doubt your publisher will want to defend against a libel suit."

Ryan looked from Iris to Tyler, then back. "All right." He turned off the audio recorder and repacked his satchel.

Tyler escorted him back to the room's door. "The most recent test results, showing 'Osiris's Journey' tested successfully, will be waiting for you Monday morning."

After he saw the reporter out, Tyler turned to Iris. He waved the stack of old test results. "Who the hell sent these to him?"

"I have no idea." Iris struggled to think, to plan. "But we'd better find out. It's obvious that someone is trying to sabotage this release."

Tyler ran a hand over his close-cropped hair. "It must have been an associate —"

"That's impossible." Iris swept her arm out. "Anderson Adventures associates are intensely loyal. No one on your payroll would have done something like this."

Tyler raised his gaze to Iris. There was pain and disappointment in his eyes. "Then who could it have been?"

CHAPTER 11

Tyler convened an emergency meeting of the Anderson Adventures executive team Sunday morning. He'd briefed everyone Friday after his meeting with Ryan Tipper and Saturday as he and Iris had waited for their flight. He'd asked Iris to attend the meeting, as well. Foster, Kayla, Donovan and Xavier joined them in the company's large conference room.

Tyler was jet-lagged. Iris must be, too, though she hid it well. They'd traveled all day Saturday from San Diego back to Columbus. Then, they'd driven straight to Anderson Adventures to email the most recent test results of "Osiris's Journey" to *The Gamer's Seat* reporter.

"The results of those tests will prove to Ryan Tipper that 'Osiris's Journey' is market ready." Tyler's gaze met those of the other executive team members, then settled on his father at the head of the table.

"I want to know one thing." Foster's voice was tight with restrained temper.

"What's that?" Tyler braced himself.

"How did this happen?" Foster pinned him with a dark, direct gaze.

That question had hung unasked in the room since the others had joined him. Now it lay on the table but Tyler wasn't any closer to answering it today than he'd been during the magazine interview.

"I don't know." Tyler felt sick. Every eye in the room seemed to be on him.

Iris leaned forward on the chair beside him. "Ty and I will review with your associates the product-testing procedure."

Foster's attention shifted from Tyler to Iris. "You think one of our associates leaked the failed test results to the media?"

Tyler heard the tension in his father's voice. "No, we don't."

"Then who did?" Foster fisted his hands on the table. "Nothing like this has ever happened before at Anderson Adventures. Ever."

"That's true, Uncle Foster." Xavier looked as troubled as he sounded. "This isn't our brightest moment. But Ty's planned an investigation to uncover the leak."

"He also was able to prevent any damage to our reputation." Donovan inclined his head to acknowledge Tyler's work.

Tyler nodded toward Iris. "With Iris's help."

"Yes." Xavier shifted on his seat. "Thank you, Iris."

Had he heard reluctance in Xavier's tone? Tyler ignored it — for now. "We'll meet with our associates tomorrow."

"You're going to meet with them although you don't think any of them had anything to do with this." Foster blew an exasperated breath. "Then what good is the meeting?"

The walls were closing in on him. "We don't think it was a deliberate act."

"You think someone emailed failed test results to the media *by accident*?" Foster's eyes widened. "That's very naive."

"Not necessarily, Foster." Donovan shrugged. "You said yourself, nothing like this has ever happened before."

"Maybe the leak wasn't an accident," Iris said. "But I don't believe it was done with malicious intent."

"Neither do I." Tyler massaged the back of his neck. "We won't know until we meet with the development team tomorrow to review the chain of command for the testing results."

"How do we know *The Gamer's Seat* is the only publication that received these documents?" Foster sat back onto his chair. "For all we know, other media outlets also received the false results and intend to publish them without warning us."

"I'm using internet alerts to monitor media coverage with references to Anderson Adventures." Iris looked to the others seated around the table. "The references to your company have been positive. It appears you're still riding the positive press from the convention. Your preorders are up and your reviews are excellent. No one has questioned your game's readiness."

"Yet." Foster's voice was tight.

His father's disappointment was a crushing weight. Would he be able to recover from this disaster? He didn't have a choice. Tyler wanted this promotion. He wanted to succeed his father as CEO of their family's company. But even more important was the fact that everyone at Anderson Adventures had worked hard to make "Osiris's Journey" a success. He wouldn't allow their efforts to be destroyed by this leak whether the information had been distributed deliberately or by accident.

Kayla tapped worriedly on the glass table. "Will you interview the associates one at a time?"

"No." Tyler shifted his attention from

Foster to his aunt. "We're going to meet with everyone who was involved with testing at once."

"We thought meeting with people individually would increase the associates' anxiety," Iris added.

How was Iris able to remain so cool and in control?

Every muscle in Tyler's body was stretched to the tearing point. "None of our associates would intentionally hurt the company. We need to investigate this leak but I don't want anyone to be uncomfortable."

"I wonder if Leslie has any interrogation techniques?" Kayla muttered the off-hand question.

"Her name's Lauren, Mom." Xavier turned to his mother, who was seated at the end of the table. "What makes you think she knows anything about interrogations?"

Kayla shrugged an elegant shoulder. "She's in HR isn't she?"

"No, she's not." Xavier frowned at his mother before turning his attention to Tyler. "We need to resolve this before the game release."

"I know." Tyler rolled his silver Cross pen between his palms. "That's why we're starting tomorrow."

Iris nodded. "It won't be a problem."

"I'll expect an update on the investigation and the media reports by end of day tomorrow." Foster stood. "If there aren't any other questions or information to be shared, let's end this meeting."

"There is one thing." Kayla raised a hand.

"What is it, Kayla?" Foster met her gaze from the other end of the table.

Kayla looked from Iris to Tyler. "We all wish this hadn't happened. The internal launch was a roaring success. It's a tough act to follow. From the reports you and Iris shared with us from the convention, you were slaying them in San Diego, as well. This matter has put a cloud over your efforts but I'm impressed and grateful for your quick and thorough actions to resolve it."

"Thank you, Ms. Anderson." Iris's voice was a soft whisper.

"It's Kayla, dear." Kayla wagged a finger at Iris.

"Thanks, Aunt Kayla." Tyler tried to smile for his aunt.

She was one of his favorite people. Ever since his mother had died, she'd done her best to ensure he had a maternal figure in his life. He wasn't going to let her down or allow this sabotage to hurt their company.

And after the investigation? What would he

do about the person who'd leaked the damaging test results?

What any good future CEO would do: fire them.

Iris let Tyler into her townhome Sunday evening. She was moving in slow motion, still weighed down by the day's events. They'd worked hard to prepare for their meeting with the "Osiris's Journey" product-development team. Her mind had short-circuited and her body felt abused. She could only imagine how Tyler felt. Waves of tension coming from him battered her like an unskilled pugilist.

"Would you like some iced tea?" Iris locked the door behind Tyler, then turned to him. His dark eyes were tired. Worry lines bracketed his full lips.

"I could use a beer." Humor eased some of the strain on his handsome features.

Iris found a smile. "Sorry. I have iced tea, lemonade and cucumber water." She set her purse on the corner table at the entrance to her living room and lowered her briefcase beside it. She toed off her shoes.

"Iced tea would be great."

Iris crossed her living room and made her way into her kitchen. Tyler followed, a warm presence at her back. She took two glasses from one of her cupboards and filled both with ice and homemade iced tea.

She presented one of the glasses to Tyler, surprised to find him so close behind her. "I could make dinner for us."

Tyler thanked her for the drink, then downed half of it. "I'm not hungry."

Neither was she. "We should eat something." She pulled open the fridge again and scanned its contents. "I'll make us a sandwich."

"Thank you." Tyler rested his hips against one of the kitchen counters.

His tall, broad-shouldered frame made her modest kitchen seem tiny but Iris didn't mind. She toasted four slices of wheat bread, then added turkey cold cuts, mozzarella cheese and a generous helping of spicy mustard. Iris kept their conversation light as she prepared dinner: weather, sports, and the pros and cons of mozzarella versus cheddar cheese. Anything to distract them from the product leak at Anderson Adventures. They needed a mental break.

"Cheddar cheese lacks imagination." Iris poured them both more iced tea and put their sandwiches on green porcelain plates. She handed Tyler his drink and a sandwich, then carried hers to the dining room table.

"And you call yourself a cheese connoisseur." Tyler's humor was forced but at least he was trying. She appreciated that.

"What's your favorite movie?" Iris took a seat at the table.

The Matrix. Tyler sat opposite her. "I love sci-fi action flicks. What's yours?"

"Hitch," Iris answered without hesitation. "I'm a sucker for romantic comedies."

"Comedy is very subjective." Tyler bit into his sandwich. A look of pleasure crossed his face.

"It's the mozzarella." She gave him a cheeky grin. "Okay. Favorite song. I have so many. For today, I'll say Alicia Keys's 'A Woman's Worth.' What's yours?"

"I don't have a favorite song." Tyler washed down another bite of sandwich with her homemade iced tea.

Iris blinked at him. "How can you not have a favorite song? Everyone has a favorite song."

Tyler shrugged. "I don't. It depends on the day and my mood."

Iris leaned into the table and lowered her voice. "I know. Your favorite song is the theme from *Star Trek,* isn't it? You can tell me. Just whisper it."

Tyler chuckled. "I don't have a favorite song. If I did, I'd tell you. I promise."

"Okay." Iris gave him a skeptical look.

"Favorite book?"

Their list of favorite things carried them through dinner. Iris was encouraged by their shared interests and excited to try some of the books and movies he'd mentioned to her. She also was determined to get him to admit to a favorite song, even if it was the theme from *2001: A Space Odyssey.* This was what she'd yearned for, someone to unwind with after a long day. Her sisters were great. But there was something extra special about a romantic interest.

"This is nice." Iris stood from the table, collecting her dishes. "I feel much more relaxed after dinner and your conversation."

"So do I." Tyler carried his empty plate and glass to the sink. "You were right about dinner. You were right about a lot of things." His voice was smooth, like the first touch of a long seduction.

"That's always nice to hear." Iris took the dishes from Tyler and loaded them into her dishwasher.

"I'm serious. I think you know I'd wanted to work with a bigger company."

"Keep bringing that up and you'll ruin the mood." Iris escorted him to her living room and silently invited him to join her on the sofa.

"Pete Kimball has never given me the high

level of customer service you're giving me." Tyler sat beside her on the sofa. "You've treated our company's product launch as more than just another contract. You've even gotten to know our associates."

Warmth filled Iris's cheeks. "It was your suggestion that I work from your office."

"But it was your warmth and caring that built those relationships."

Tyler's praise was gratifying even as it made her uncomfortable. "I'm glad you're satisfied with my work."

"Not just satisfied." His dark eyes searched hers. "I couldn't have gotten this far without you. And now with this crisis, I'm glad you're at my side."

"We're in this together."

Tyler watched Iris's lips form the words. He, Xavier and Donovan had been a team for years. They'd helped each other get through college. They'd worked on projects together at Anderson Adventures. But there was something so erotic about the image of him and Iris being a team. It was mesmerizing, hypnotizing. Tyler leaned toward Iris, his eyes still on her lips. He groaned as he brought his mouth to hers. He tasted her sweetness. Swallowed her sigh. He tightened his arms around her, shifting even closer. Her warmth wrapped him like a caress. He released her lips and buried his face in the curve of her neck. He breathed her in. Citrus and vanilla filled his lungs and clouded his mind. Her scent transported him to a darkened room in a posh hotel where he'd finally given in to what he wanted.

"Iris." He whispered her name.

"Yes, Ty?" Her voice was more sigh than words.

Tyler's body stirred. He lifted his head and gazed down into her steamy coffee eyes. "Thank God I found you."

Her eyes softened. Iris swayed toward him. She covered his mouth with her own as though needing to drink his declaration. Her fingernails bore into the muscles of his back. Desire sparking inside him blazed white-hot. His mouth no longer tasted and explored. It demanded and took. He wanted to watch her. He needed to feel her. He ached to taste her — all at once.

Tyler tore his mouth free. "You're going to kill me."

"You're doing the same." Iris's laugh was soft and shaky. "At least I'll die happy."

Am I dreaming? Could it possibly be true that the computer nerd had found a woman who was brilliant, beautiful and crazy for him? "I couldn't be any happier."

Her lips curved into a wicked smile. "Give me a moment."

His laughter ended on a groan as her hands moved over his torso. Iris's fingers trembled as she plucked at his shirt's buttons. Tyler brushed her hands aside to help her. He unfastened his shirt, then took her back into his embrace. Iris slipped her soft, slim hands beneath his shirt and caressed his bare chest. Her touch was magic, stirring a desire in him more potent and powerful than anything he'd felt before.

"So hard. So strong. A fantasy." She moaned the words into his ear.

Tyler's muscles shook with need. "I dreamed of you before I knew you."

He gave her one last hard kiss, then gathered her into his arms. He looked down into her startled eyes. "Bed?"

With her directions, he made quick work of carrying her up the stairs and to her bedroom. The entire time, Iris licked, kissed and caressed him, adding to the desire already raging through his blood. He wanted her now. He wanted to be on her, in her, around her.

Tyler crossed into her room. In his peripheral vision, he had an impression of gold and blue, and lots of books. But his focus remained on the queen-size bed dominating the space. He released Iris beside it. With haste, he helped her remove her clothes as she helped him. Moments later, they stood nude.

Tyler cupped the side of her breast in his palm. "Lovely."

"You, too." Iris fixed her gaze on his torso. She raked her fingertips from his chest to his hips. His muscle flexed toward her.

Somehow they ended up on the bed. She sprawled on top of him like a soft, light blanket. Tyler caught her beautiful face between his hands and deepened their kiss. He'd had a dream like this once. It had come true in San Diego and again now.

He rolled them over, balancing on top of her. "Let me love you."

Iris smiled in a silent invitation to ecstasy. Tyler smiled back, eager to love every inch of her. Hoping to reach her heart.

Iris caught her breath. All she knew was this man, his touch and the magic he made with her body. Tyler licked his way down her neck. Iris quivered. His mouth moved slowly over her breast. Her nipples tightened. His lips wrapped around its tip. Her torso arched. She offered him more of her. Tyler released her to move farther down her body. A trail of heat followed where he led, melting her insides.

Her mind went blank. "You're making me crazy."

"I'm already there."

His hands massaged her breasts, pinching her nipples as his mouth explored her navel. Iris closed her eyes, lost in sensation. She pressed her breasts into his palms and squeezed his hands. Tyler traveled lower. He stopped here and tasted her. There, he placed a kiss. The muscles in her abdomen fluttered and tightened. He blew a breath over the curls that masked her treasure. Iris dampened. Tyler drew his fingers through her nest. She arched from the mattress. Her core flooded with moisture.

"Ty." She puffed his name on a breath.

"Let me love you." His whisper was a surge of electricity, streaming from the crown of her head to the flesh eager and yearning between her thighs.

"Yes." Had she begged? She was willing to.

Tyler gathered her hips and carried them to his mouth. He kissed her.

Ecstasy tore through her. It shocked her heart and stole her breath. Iris drove her head into the pillow. She gritted her teeth to keep from screaming her pleasure. Her hips rocked and twisted. Tyler held her in place with his hands, kissing her deeper with his lips and his tongue. Fulfilling his promise to love her, cherish her. Iris grew hotter. Her muscles strained tighter. Her hips lifted higher. Blood roared in her ears. Her heart thundered in her chest. Too soon her desire burst and her body rocked as though ready to tear apart. She stiffened, then collapsed in Tyler's hands.

Tyler released her. Slowly, she opened her eyes. She found him taking a condom from his wallet.

"Let me." Iris dragged herself to her knees and took the condom from him. She pressed her hand to his chest, urging him to the mattress. A thin sheen of perspiration gleamed on his muscles. His heart beat against her palm. She straddled him, then took him into her mouth. She sucked him once, twice, thrice before rolling the condom up his thick, rigid length. She clenched with anticipation of his filling her.

"Now let *me* love *you.*" Iris leaned forward to kiss him. She shivered as the hair on his pectorals teased her nipples.

She stroked her tongue across the seam of his mouth, teasing him. He opened for her, allowing her to deepen their kiss. Soon the sweet ache of desire awakened again. Iris straightened. The look in his eyes made her burn hotter. She was on fire for this man.

Iris lifted her hips. She watched Tyler as she took him inside her. His eyes flared with hunger as she lowered herself onto him slowly, ever so slowly. Feeling all of him stretching all of her. Iris's back arched as the thrill of possession shivered through her. Tyler reached for her, gripping her hips as his erection pressed up into her, filling her completely. Iris gasped, closing her eyes as sensation all but overwhelmed her.

Tyler worked her hips, guiding them to a rhythm that multiplied the pleasure. It was like pleasure in stereo. His length stroked her, a wicked caress that rocked her hips deeper and faster. His hands moved over her sides, rising past her waist and up her torso to cup her breasts. Iris arched her back, pressing her nipples into his palms. Tyler caressed them, kneaded them. Iris's desire grew more and more urgent.

"Can't think." She leaned forward, reclaiming Tyler's gaze.

"Not supposed to." Tyler lowered his hands. He lifted his head and drew her nipple into his mouth.

Iris gasped, rubbing her spot against him. Tyler slipped his fingers between them and found her. Iris worked herself against his touch even as he moved inside her. Her muscles strained. The pleasure grew sharper, tighter, deeper. Tyler's power lifted her higher. She pressed down on him again and again. Her muscles wrapped tighter and tighter — until she shattered.

Tyler rolled over and covered her. His hips moved with hers, his rhythm fast and deep, echoing her pulse. Then with one final powerful thrust, his climax joined with hers.

Tyler was back in the associates' lounge Monday morning. He scanned the large cheerfully decorated room. The stakes were much higher since the last time he'd been at a meeting in this room. Someone's job was at risk.

"If you don't think any of us are responsible for the leak, what are we doing here?" Ted, the IT analyst, seemed to be the spokesperson for the ten-member design team assigned to "Osiris's Journey."

"We don't think it was a malicious leak." Tyler stood to address the team. "Maybe the person meant to send the *positive* test results to the e-zine."

"Or he or she didn't mean to send test results outside of the company at all." Iris spoke from an armchair. "This whole thing could have been an accident."

Ted snorted. "That's naive."

His father had said the same thing. *Am I*

being naive? But why would anyone sabotage the success of a project on which they'd worked so long and hard?

"The fact is we don't know how Tipper got his hands on a copy of the earlier results." Tyler couldn't control his urge to pace the room any longer. "But no one believes anyone at Anderson Adventures would send it to him, intending to harm the company. What would be the motive?"

Malek Gifford, a game designer, looked from Iris to Tyler. His thin dark features were tense. "How are you going to find the leak?"

"Let's go over the test procedures again." Tyler paced as Ted, Malek and others reviewed in painful detail each step of the testing process. He filled in their blanks with his specific responsibilities.

By the end of the nearly hour-long session, their investigation hadn't garnered anything out of the ordinary. Everyone had followed procedure. No one had taken any shortcuts. If anything, their team had taken extra precautions to safeguard the sensitive information.

"Thanks for coming to talk with us like this rather than sneaking around behind our backs and checking our emails." Ted stretched his legs in front of him, and crossed his arms and ankles.

"I don't want it to come to that." A weight had settled on Tyler's shoulders.

Ted nodded. "That's good to know."

"But if we don't learn who's behind the leak, we won't have a choice." Tyler regretted an email search was beginning to look like a real possibility.

"Fair enough." Ted adjusted his glasses on the bridge of his nose.

Ever since the internal launch, his interactions with associates had been improving. He couldn't walk across the parking lot without someone greeting him or walk down the hallway without someone asking about his day. Would this leak damage his new camaraderie in addition to his father's trust in him?

Tyler faced the room one last time. "If anyone has anything they'd like to add, call me and we can speak in confidence."

Malek shrugged. "Ty, I'm telling you, it wasn't us."

Tyler was relieved that his team hadn't been involved. But he was disappointed that he hadn't turned up any useful information. Now he had to figure out what his next step was going to be.

The one thing he *was* sure about right

now was that he was glad Iris was by his side.

"What do you think?" Tyler walked with Iris back to his office after the meeting. He stood aside, allowing her to precede him into the room before shutting the door behind them.

"I still don't think any of them did it." Iris turned to him. Her cool-blue, short-sleeved blouse and pencil-thin navy skirt made her look both professional and sexy.

"Neither do I." Tyler shoved his hands deep into the front pockets of his black Dockers.

"They were forthcoming, relaxed, direct. They didn't seem to have anything to hide."

"I know. Dammit." Tyler paced his office, searching for inspiration. He was like a rat in a maze, going in circles without a sense of direction. There was no way out.

"What do we do now?" Iris's question brought his spinning thoughts to a halt.

Tyler checked his watch. It was after ten o'clock. "I need to give my father an update on the investigation by the end of the day. I hope someone calls me for that confidential chat before then."

"What will you do when you get that call?"

"It depends on the reason the old test results were leaked." Tyler shrugged. "It may not have been a malicious act but that doesn't change the fact that confidential information was sent to the media."

Iris's elegant features reflected her concern. "I can't wait to put this whole episode behind us. It's cast a shadow over the good work you've done."

"The good work *we've* done." Tyler crossed the room to take her hand. "We're a team, remember?"

"A darn good one." Iris squeezed his hand before slipping hers free. "I'd better finish that social media policy. You're going to need a full-time person to handle your presence. We're getting a lot of likes on Facebook and retweets on Twitter."

"Great." Whatever that meant.

Iris opened his office door, then nudged the doorstop into place with her foot. "Call me if you need me."

"You do the same." Tyler watched Iris disappear beyond his door.

If he called her every time he needed her, he'd be on the phone every minute of the day. How had he come to need her that much in just three short months? Was it a good thing — or not?

Iris exhaled, kicking off her shoes and carrying the Chinese-food takeout into her kitchen Monday evening. Their traditional family dinner was Wednesday but Tyler was working late and she really needed to see her sisters tonight. That's why she'd sent the 911 — teriyaki chicken and veggies at 6 text message on her way home. Rose and Lily should arrive any minute.

She set the dining room table before transferring the chicken and vegetables to a serving bowl and settling that within easy reach of the three place settings. The doorbell rang. Iris hurried to answer it.

She checked the peephole before pulling open her front door to welcome Rose and Lily. "Did you two drive over together?"

Rose crossed the threshold and kissed Iris's cheek. "No, we just arrived at the same time."

Lily squeezed in behind Rose and locked the front door. She turned to Iris with a smile but her cocoa eyes were watchful. It wasn't every day that the sisters sent each other 911 texts. "Dinner smells terrific."

"It's not as good as your cooking." Iris leaned down to kiss her older — but significantly shorter — sister on the cheek. "Thanks for coming." She led the way to the dining area.

"Let's talk and eat. I'm hungry and curious." Rose left her purse on a chair at the dining table and began serving herself. She then passed the bowl to Lily. "What's happened?"

Iris took a deep breath. "Anderson Adventures has a leak."

Lily tilted her head. "What kind of leak?"

"The 'someone sent damaging information to the press' kind." Iris accepted the serving bowl as she brought her sisters up to date.

She kept her explanation brief. Her sisters didn't need to know Tyler had called her his good-luck charm or that he made her feel like an accomplished, creative, desirable woman.

Or that they'd made love twice in one night while attending an industry convention as consultant and client. *Yikes!*

Rose lowered her knife and fork to pin Iris with an incredulous look. "An Anderson Adventures employee sent the failed test results to the media? Are you kidding me?"

"Those test results were outdated." Iris shook her head. " 'Osiris's Journey' has passed two recent tests with flying colors."

"That just makes it worse." Rose was adamant. "A trusted employee *knowingly* sent damaging and erroneous information to the press."

Iris lifted her hand, palm out. "We don't

think the leak came from an Anderson Adventures associate."

Rose shrugged. "Just because you think you can trust someone doesn't mean you can."

Iris sighed. "Does every conversation have to lead back to Ben?"

"Do you have any leads on who might have sent the information?" Lily's quiet question put a cork in Iris's rising temper.

"None." Iris stared at her plate of untouched food. "One of the worst things about this is that I was completely blind-sided."

"You see." Rose pointed her table knife toward Iris. "I knew you shouldn't have taken this account. It's too much for you."

Iris frowned. "What do you mean it's too much for me?"

"It's a lot for you to handle," Rose replied. "You're a one-woman show."

Iris was offended, though she tried to hide it. "What could a bigger firm do that I didn't?"

Rose shook her head as she forked up more vegetables. "I'm not knocking your firm. I'm just telling you the reason you were blindsided by this debacle is that you're not equipped to handle a project this big."

"You still haven't told me what a bigger firm would've done." Iris guarded her tone.

Lily gave Rose a quelling look. "There isn't anything a bigger firm would've done that you didn't do."

"Oh, that's fine for you to say." Rose waved her fork at Lily. "You're the one who got her into this mess."

"You're welcome." Lily stabbed a broccoli spear covered with teriyaki sauce. "But it's pointless to argue now whether Iris's firm is equipped to handle unanticipated problems. The question now is what should Iris do?"

"I don't know what to do. I'm fresh out of ideas." Iris went back to pushing her food around her plate.

Rose shifted in her seat to look at her. "You need to explain to Tyler Anderson that you're out of your league."

"I was hoping for more constructive advice." Every word from her sister's mouth added to Iris's self-doubts.

"The leak may just be a symptom of the problem." Lily's tone was pensive. "The real question is what was the point of the leak? Was it to hurt Anderson Adventures, Tyler Anderson or Iris?"

Iris frowned. "What do you mean?"

Lily shrugged her narrow shoulders. "To figure out who leaked the test results, you need to identify the reason that information was leaked. Who's trying to hurt whom?"

Iris stared at her sister. "I hadn't considered that. Maybe someone *is* out to get Ty."

"Find the saboteur before he or she does more damage." Lily sipped her ice water. "And let me know what I can do to help."

Rose sniffed. "By helping her land this Anderson Adventures account, I think you've done enough."

Iris arched a brow at her elder sister. "Rose, what do I need to do to prove myself to you?"

Rose's dark eyes dimmed with concern. "You don't have to prove anything to me. I just don't want you to be disappointed."

Iris lifted her chin. "The only way I'd be disappointed is if I didn't try. And Ty has worked too hard to lose everything now."

"Ty?" Rose's winged eyebrows rose. "What about you?"

"Iris, are you falling in love with Ty Anderson?" Lily searched Iris's expression.

Iris hesitated. "I think I am."

Rose gaped. "You're kidding, aren't you?"

Iris turned to Lily. "I know it wasn't smart —"

"You're right. It wasn't." Rose rubbed her temples as though her head was beginning to ache.

Iris ignored her eldest sister's comment. "I couldn't help myself. He's different from the men I usually meet. There's something so sexy about the way he's unaware of his appeal."

Lily reached over to cup Iris's hand. "How does he feel about you?"

"I think he has feelings for me, too." Iris met Rose's gaze. "He was cautious about me at first. But now he's realized I'm a competent professional."

"So he says." Rose shook her head. "Men, you can't trust them."

"This one trusts me." Iris thought of the night she and Tyler had spent together in San Diego. He made her feel mysterious, desirable, beautiful. Cherished.

"Be careful, Iris." Lily looked worried. "I don't want you to be hurt."

"I won't be." Iris was confident. "I know it's not smart to mix business and pleasure. But you can't always choose the time and place you fall in love."

CHAPTER 12

"How did it go?" Xavier settled onto one of the gray guest chairs in Tyler's office. Donovan claimed the other.

Tyler glanced at his watch. It was just after six o'clock on one of the longest Mondays in world history. He wished he'd left with Iris when she'd stopped by his office to say good-night. He'd been more focused on work and what he would say to his father.

Tyler rubbed the back of his neck, easing the knots that were straining those muscles. "About as well as could be expected."

"Ouch." Donovan gave him an empathetic look. "Is Foster going to delay his retirement again?"

"Probably." His father's plan to promote Tyler to chief executive officer so Foster could retire probably had taken a serious hit after this company leak. Would Foster make good on his threat to look outside the company for his successor? Tyler glanced at his empty coffee cup. Was it too late to make a fresh pot and pour himself a refill?

Donovan settled his left ankle on his right knee. "Is there anything we can do?"

"Can you turn back time?" Tyler visualized again the associates who'd gathered with him in the lounge nine hours earlier: Ted, Malek and the rest of his team. "There's no way anyone can convince me our associates had anything to do with this."

"If not them, then who?" Donovan spread his hands.

Tyler slouched back on his chair. "We could drive ourselves crazy, going around and around with that question."

Xavier looked from Donovan to Tyler. "If we rule out everyone on the inside, who's left?"

Donovan shifted on his seat to face Xavier. "Say what's on your mind, X."

Xavier shrugged his shoulders under his dark green shirt. "What do we know about Iris?"

Tyler tensed. Was Xavier accusing Iris of being the leak? "My father asked me to contact her."

"That's a pretty strong professional reference, if you ask me." Donovan's tone was dry.

"Why would she try to damage the release

she's working on?" Tyler hadn't felt this violent toward his cousin since they were twelve.

"Maybe someone offered her money." Xavier settled his hands on the arms of his chair.

Donovan's eyes widened. "*We* offered her money."

"Iris would never accept a bribe to betray a client." Tyler would bet everything he had on that. She had too much integrity. "Besides, she doesn't have access to the tests or their results. I've never shown her any of the documents."

"She might have gotten them from someone else." Xavier shrugged again.

"Which brings us back to the theory that an associate leaked sensitive information to an outside party." Tyler shook his head. "I don't believe our people would do that."

Nor do I believe Iris would betray our trust.

"Where is this coming from, X?" Donovan looked at the vice president of finance as though he'd never seen him before. "This doesn't sound like you."

Tyler agreed. "You usually have more than speculation before you make accusations."

Xavier met Tyler's eyes. "I know you have a thing for her."

Donovan tossed him a grin. "Good choice,

by the way."

Tyler tensed. "My attraction to Iris isn't clouding my judgment."

"Good." Donovan nodded decisively. "Then we don't have anything to worry about."

"We have a big issue." Xavier looked at Donovan. "The leak still hasn't been found."

"I've asked IT to search our email system to identify the account that sent the tests to Tipper." Tyler didn't want to invade his associates' privacy but what else could he do? He needed to get to the bottom of this.

"I know the decision wasn't an easy one for you." Donovan sounded sympathetic. "Especially since this task will take them away from the final adjustments to 'Osiris's Journey' before the release."

"How long will the search take?" Xavier asked.

Tyler shook his head. "We're just looking for transmissions between *The Gamer's Seat* and Anderson Adventures. I should have something by tomorrow afternoon."

"Are they checking every account?" It was obvious his cousin wanted to know whether Iris's account was included in the search.

Tyler considered Xavier. These accusations were out of character. "Every account on the network."

"Then for better and worse, this should be over tomorrow." Xavier stood.

Donovan rose from his chair, as well. He looked concerned. "Don't stay too late. There's nothing we can do until tomorrow."

"I'll leave soon." Tyler watched them walk through his door.

Yes, for better and worse, they'd have an answer to the mystery of the security breach tomorrow. Knowing who had leaked the test results would help determine what procedures should be put in place to ensure it never happened again. At the same time, the leak was someone who had betrayed their trust. How would the identity of the traitor affect their company?

Xavier seemed to think Iris had something to do with the leak. The idea was absurd. For one thing, a failed launch for "Osiris's Journey" would reflect poorly on her company. For another, Iris didn't have access to the test results. She couldn't be responsible for the leak. Tyler wasn't that poor a judge of character.

Iris paced her living room Monday night. So many questions bombarded her mind: Who'd leaked the old test results to *The Gamer's Seat*? When had he or she contacted the reporter? What made him think he could get away with something like this? Most important, why would someone try to hurt Anderson Adventures?

Iris dropped onto her sofa, resting her head on its back. Tyler had seemed devastated when she'd gone to his office to say good-night. He hadn't called to tell her how his update with Foster had gone. That couldn't be a good sign.

She sat forward, cupping her face in her palms. In her mind's eye, she pictured the ten members of the product-development team and Sherry as they sat in the associates' lounge eleven hours ago. No one had looked, sounded or acted guilty. Instead, they'd been surprised and angry. Someone had leaked damaging information about their game. They were personally and professionally insulted.

She sat up. Speaking with Rose and Lily had helped some but Iris needed another sounding board. She glanced at the clock on her cable box. It was just after 8:00 p.m. Was Tyler home? Iris shook her head. They'd been debating, dissecting and discussing the situation since Friday. She needed a fresh perspective. Iris grabbed her cordless phone and punched in Cathy's number.

"Hello?" Her friend answered on the third ring.

"Are you busy? I need to pick your brain."

"Shoot. You can have whatever's left." In the background, the sound of Cathy's television suddenly silenced.

Iris stood to pace her living room again as she brought Cathy up to date on the Anderson Adventures leak.

"So you don't think it was an inside job." Cathy made the statement after a brief pause.

"No, neither Ty nor I believe an associate was involved." Iris lowered herself onto her sofa. "I don't think the executive leadership believes it was someone in their company, either."

"Then it was someone on the outside."

"How do I figure out who did it?"

"I can think of one person." Cathy's voice was dry.

"Pete Kimball." Iris sighed. "I thought of him, too. But what would he get from hurting Anderson Adventures? What have they ever done to him?"

"They hired you." Cathy's response was quick and decisive.

"Be serious." Iris leaned back on the sofa. She stared blindly across the room, imaging Cathy sitting on her own sofa in her own living room.

"I am." Her friend certainly sounded serious. "He lied to Ty Anderson about the reason you left RGB, remember? He's capable of sabotaging their new release."

"The jerk." She'd never forget Pete Kimball's lies. "But someone within Anderson Adventures would still need to send Kimball the test results."

"Kimball has worked with Anderson Adventures before. He knows the employees. He probably has their email addresses and direct phone numbers." Cathy's words came faster as she fleshed out her scenario. "He could have called someone, made up some story about the reason he needed the documents, then casually asked for them."

Iris considered her friend's theory. It had legs. "You have a point. But how could this be about me?"

"Kimball's not happy that you got the account. He's probably trying to make you look bad."

Iris wouldn't put it past the egotistical marketing executive. She got to her feet, then wandered her living room. "This leak has shaken me more than I would've thought. Maybe Rose is right. Maybe I've taken on more than I can handle."

Cathy sighed. "Your sisters love you very much. They're protective of you, and I understand that. But Rose is wrong. You've already proven with the work you've done for Anderson that you can handle these types of projects."

A part of Iris agreed with her friend. Then why did she feel so far out of her element? "I can handle individual projects but can I handle a campaign?"

"Yes. And I'm not just saying that because you've hired me to design Anderson's marketing collateral." Cathy sighed again. "Now put on your big-girl pants and find out who's trying to sabotage your client."

Iris gave a dry chuckle. "My favorite thing about you is your empathetic pep talks."

Cathy harrumphed. "Don't be such a wimp. You said Lily told you to find the saboteur. She's right. Don't overlook Kimball."

Iris scowled. "He's at the top of my list."

Tuesday morning, Iris stormed past Peter Kimball's secretary and shoved open the marketing executive's office door.

The curvy, middle-aged woman dithered in Iris's wake. "Pete, I'm sorry. I tried to stop her but she just pushed past me."

Peter continued typing at his laptop before

looking up at his secretary. "That's all right, Florence. I think the whole industry is aware that Ms. Beharie's manners leave a lot to be desired."

"They certainly do." Florence's small powder-blue eyes glared up at Iris. "Should I escort her out?"

"Good luck with that." Iris arched an eyebrow. The other woman was more than a head shorter than her. "I'm not leaving until I'm ready to go."

Peter waved his hand dismissively. "Don't worry. Ms. Beharie will be ready to leave soon. Please close the door on your way out."

Florence hesitated, obviously torn between staying and going. "Let me know if you want me to call security." With a final glare, the older woman spun on her heel, then slammed the door shut behind her.

"What can I do for you, Iris?" Peter's question drew Iris's attention back to him.

"You can tell me who sent you the first results from 'Osiris's Journey' 's product testing."

"What are you talking about?" His expression of confusion was perfectly nuanced. If Iris didn't know better she'd believe his act. It was the ninth day of June. "Osiris's Journey" would launch in a month. She didn't have time for this.

Peter sat in an overstuffed big crimson leather chair behind a large, old fashioned mahogany desk. His pale pink shirt highlighted his cold gray eyes and heavily tanned features.

Iris settled her hands on her hips. "You sent the file to *The Gamer's Seat* to hurt Anderson Adventures' product launch. But your plan didn't work."

Peter's eyes widened with surprise, then he threw his head back and roared with laughter. "Did someone leak damaging information to the media before your client's product launch?"

She fisted her hands at her sides. "You did."

"I assure you I did not." Peter shook his head, still laughing. "But this is rich. Too good to be true."

Iris narrowed her eyes at her rival. "Why should I believe you?"

"I'm not asking you to." Peter wiped the tears of hilarity from his eyes. "Oh, I bet Foster Anderson is royally pissed that Ty hired you now."

Iris swallowed, trying to dislodge the ball of fear stuck in her throat. Peter looked and sounded genuinely amused. Could he be telling the truth? *Impossible.*

"You're not going to get away with this." She regarded Peter with contempt as he continued his hyena impersonation.

"How did you find out about the leak?" His gray eyes gleamed with spite and satisfaction. "Was it an internet alert? Or maybe it was a phone call from the press?"

Iris had checked her internet alerts prior to storming Kimball & Associates' gates. Luckily, Anderson Adventures and "Osiris's Journey" were still riding positive press from the Electronic Gaming Convention.

"When did you get the document?" She pinned him with a steely stare.

"What makes you think I leaked the file?" Peter's humor faded only slightly.

"Because you're a spiteful little man." Iris allowed her disdain for her competitor to show. "Ty Anderson awarded the campaign to me —"

"And they got what they paid for."

"You were so jealous you lied about the events that led to my leaving RGB."

"Everything's fair in marketing and war." Peter took a deep drink of coffee from his ceramic mug. His movements were easy and relaxed.

Iris wanted to slap the mug from his hand. "You're capable of schmoozing one of your inside contacts into sending you the old test results, then passing those documents to the media as though they were the most recent product tests."

Peter almost choked on a mouthful of coffee. Almost, but not quite. More's the pity. "You just keep telling yourself that, Iris. Maybe you'll eventually be able to convince yourself that's what happened."

Either Peter was telling the truth or he had Sir Anthony Hopkins–sized acting chops. Iris shook her head. He had to be lying. "What did you hope to achieve? Were you trying to hurt me or Anderson Adventures?"

Peter shook his head as though in pity. "Until you told me, I had no idea that Anderson Adventures had a security breach."

"You're lying."

"This is the first time anything like that has ever happened at that company. And it happened on your watch." Peter grinned with glee. "How does that feel?"

"It will give me the greatest satisfaction to tell them you're the one behind this leak."

"You'd be lying." Peter sobered. "I told you from the beginning that you're out of your league with this client."

"The campaign was progressing well before you played your games."

"This would never have happened if I'd been on the account." Peter sat forward, reaching for his phone. "Should I call Ty to give him my condolences?"

Iris's heart raced as her anger grew. "Just remember, Pete, payback's a bitch."

"You're out of your league, little girl." Peter crossed his legs and leaned back in chair. "Way out of your league."

Iris racked her brain to come up with some way to trick Peter into confessing but nothing came to mind. It was obvious she wasn't going to get him to admit to his involvement in the security breach.

She clenched her teeth and turned toward the door. "I still have the account, old man."

She'd find another way to fix this. Not only was her reputation on the line but this leak threatened Tyler's chances of succeeding his father at the family company's helm. With any luck, Tyler would receive the results of the email investigation today and they could start to put the matter behind them. She kept her fingers crossed.

Iris arrived at Anderson Adventures shortly after 10:00 a.m. Tuesday. She exchanged a brief but cheery good-morning with Sherry. She was still distracted by her earlier exchange with Peter Kimball. What would

Tyler think about her theory?

She stopped in his doorway before continuing to her conference room. Tyler sat at his desk. Iris took a moment to enjoy looking at him. He was so handsome. His broad shoulders were covered in a copper pullover. He stared contemplatively at his computer screen. Lost in thought, he seemed miles away.

She knocked tentatively on the door. "Ty? Do you have a moment?"

"Where have you been?" He seemed to be looking through her. His question wasn't accusatory. Instead he sounded almost resigned.

This morning, she'd wanted to bring him a resolution to this crisis. She'd hoped to take away his troubles. Instead, she could only offer him more questions.

"I went to speak with Pete Kimball." Iris frowned. "Didn't you get my message?"

"Close the door, Iris."

She nudged the block of wood out from under the door, frowning at Tyler's stiff tone. "This must be serious."

"I got your message." Tyler took his time saving his computer file, then turned to face her. "But I don't understand why you went to speak with him."

Iris walked farther into the room. There

was a chill in the air. And she was getting a weird vibe from him.

"I think Kimball is behind our security breach." Iris lowered herself onto one of Tyler's guest chairs.

Tyler gave her a skeptical look. "Why do you think that?"

What was going on with him? He didn't seem or sound like the friend and colleague to whom she'd bid good-night yesterday, much less the lover with whom she'd spent the night during the convention in San Diego.

Iris hesitated. "He was unhappy when he didn't get your product launch. I think convincing someone on your team to email the old test results to him, then leaking that information to the media, is his way of getting back at us."

"Who did he convince to help him?"

"We'll know once you get the results of the email investigation."

Tyler was silent for several seconds. The look in his ebony eyes was distant, considering. Cool. "I have the results. They came earlier than expected."

Her heart leaped. This was good news. It meant the mystery was over. But it was also bad news. Now they'd know who'd broken their trust. Over the past three months, she'd gotten to know several of the Anderson Adventures associates well. She hoped with all her heart it hadn't been any of them.

Iris sat straighter on the chair, bracing herself for the news. "Who was it?"

Tyler held her gaze as though trying to read her mind. "It was you, Iris. You were the leak."

CHAPTER 13

He was serious.

Iris's head spun as though she were in a tire, racing down a hill. Too fast. Her ears were buzzing. She couldn't catch her breath. Her heart thundered as though it would burst from her chest.

"What are you talking about?" She gasped the question. Her voice sounded so far away.

"The search of our email system found this transmission." Tyler slid a sheet of paper across the glass surface of his desk.

Iris leaned forward. Her hand shook as she accepted the document. The transmission was from her email account at Anderson Adventures to Ryan Tipper at *The Gamer's Seat.* Iris looked up at Tyler in shock. His face remained expressionless.

Does he really believe me capable of this?

She returned her attention to the email printout. It was sent at 11:53 a.m. on May 21, about two weeks before the industry convention in San Diego. She struggled to read it as the paper shook in her grasp, causing the words to bounce before her eyes. The message claimed that she'd attached a pdf of the "Osiris's Journey" test results because she wanted Tipper to expose "the fraud Anderson Adventures was about to perpetrate on consumers."

I'm in the middle of a nightmare.

"This doesn't even sound like me." She hadn't realized she'd said the words out loud until Tyler spoke.

"What do you mean?"

She looked into his cold eyes. He was so still, so watchful. *I'm on trial.* "I didn't send this."

"It was sent from your computer through your email account."

"Then someone else used my computer and my account to send this message."

"Who?"

Iris spread her hands. She struggled to control her voice despite her increasing agitation. "I don't know, Ty. All I do know is that *I* didn't send this."

Tyler finally moved, leaning into his desk to hold Iris's gaze. "Only five people have key cards that can access all of the offices in this building: my father, my aunt, Xavier, Donovan and me. Are you accusing one of us of framing you?"

"I'm not accusing anyone." Iris shook the sheet of paper as she was forced to repeat herself for the third time. "I'm telling you this isn't me."

"Even if someone else did manage to gain key-card access to your office, how would they get into your password-protected email system?"

Her heart dropped. "I don't always remember to lock my computer."

"Convenient." Tyler sat back on his chair.

That hurt.

"I'm not lying." And if he had any trust in her, he'd know that. Her emotions shifted from fear to anger. Iris stood. "When we made love, you told me you trusted me. What's changed now that we have our clothes on?"

Tyler rose, as well. A wide range of emotions moved across his features: disappointment, confusion, sorrow and anger. He was experiencing the same feelings she was.

He gestured toward the sheet she'd unknowingly crushed in her fist. "I can't deny the evidence staring me in the face."

"I signed a contract with you to produce two successful product launches. Why would I jeopardize my own project?"

"I was hoping you'd tell me."

"I wouldn't. I didn't." Iris held his gaze. She pushed the words past the lump burning her throat. "I'm asking you to believe me. Trust me, Ty."

Tyler searched her eyes. Iris held her breath as he looked deep inside her. She didn't flinch, didn't look away. Seconds ticked by building toward a minute, perhaps two. She held her ground, firm in the knowledge of the truth; she hadn't betrayed him. She wasn't the leak. Would he have faith in her?

Vulnerability flashed in his eyes before they hardened. "You're not giving me anything to support your innocence."

He'd torn another piece of her heart. "All I have is my word."

"I don't have the luxury of ignoring the evidence. I have to protect Anderson Adventures and our seventy associates."

"Ty, you know me. You must know I'm not capable of this."

"We traced the leak back to you." Tyler spoke as though he hadn't heard her. "Under the circumstances, I have to ask you to leave. Immediately."

His voice was so cold, emotionless. It was as though he was talking to a stranger. He was treating her like one. Her mind flashed back to the night they'd made love more than once. She clung desperately to her anger to keep from being sick.

"You can't possibly believe I'd jeopardize my own contract."

"If you leave now, we can avoid criminal charges."

Iris froze. "Criminal —"

"We'll pack your belongings and have them delivered to you."

Iris could only stare at him. She'd run out of arguments with which to defend herself. She tried but couldn't collect her thoughts. The pain of this moment was a thousand times worse than the betrayal she'd experienced at RGB Inc. She'd seen that moment coming. But Tyler had blindsided her completely.

I trust you. He'd given her that gift in a dark hotel room. In the light of day, he'd taken it back.

Iris swallowed the lump in her throat. "I'll return the partial payment you gave me when we signed our contract."

"Keep it. It's for the services you provided."

Don't cry. Don't cry. Don't you dare cry.

"That's not necessary." All she'd asked for was his trust. He couldn't give her that; she wouldn't take his money. Iris turned to leave.

Don't cry. Don't cry.

She strode through the executive suite, back straight, shoulders squared and eyes dry, if itchy. Her stride faltered as she approached Sherry's desk. She'd miss the warm, cheerful woman. With an effort, she pasted on a smile.

"Hey, Iris. Where are you off to?" Sherry's voice was as welcoming as ever. News of Iris's alleged betrayal must not have made it through the company's grapevine yet. *Thank goodness.*

"Home." Her voice wobbled.

"Are you okay?" Sherry looked closely at Iris as she passed the front desk.

"No."

"I'm sorry, dear. Feel better." Sherry's kind words almost tugged loose her self-control.

Mercifully, Iris made it to the door. She sent Sherry one last smile before leaving.

Whoever framed her had taken so much more from her than a project and some money. They'd taken her reputation, budding friendships and the man with whom she was beginning to fall in love, and for what? No matter how long it took, she'd get the answer to that question.

Iris exited Anderson Adventures and crossed the parking lot to her car. Somehow she'd prove to Tyler that she hadn't been the leak. She'd make him realize he could trust her. Doing that would at least salvage their professional relationship. But what about their personal one? Iris climbed into her car and finally let her tears fall. They were hot rivers of sorrow racing down her cheeks.

Face it, Iris. You and Ty never had a personal relationship. You imagined it.

She slapped her tears away, took a deep breath, then started her car. *How could Ty love me and truly believe I could commit such a despicable act?*

An hour later, Tyler knocked on Xavier's office door. In his opposite hand, he gripped the printout of the report Ted had just given him.

"Ty, come in." Xavier saved his computer file, locked his system, then turned to Tyler. "How did it go with Iris? Did she tell you why she sent the email?"

"She said she didn't." Ty took one of the chairs in front of Xavier's desk.

His cousin shrugged his shoulders. "I guess that's to be expected. Lauren suspected her right away. I'm sorry."

"What was it about Iris that made Lauren suspicious?" The report in Tyler's hands weighed heavy on his heart.

"I don't know. Maybe it's because Iris is the only outsider and we all agreed one of our associates couldn't have leaked the information."

"On a hunch, I asked Ted to run a report on the key-card access to Iris's office for the day she's supposed to have sent the email to Tipper." Tyler glanced at the sheet of paper in his hand. "Iris is adamant about her innocence and I can't believe she'd jeopardize her own project."

"Computers don't lie, Ty. You of all people know that."

"That's true," Tyler agreed. "But they don't always tell the entire story, either."

"What did you learn?" Xavier gestured toward the report.

Tyler skimmed the report for the fifth time. He could probably recite the whole thing from memory. "I asked Ted to check the small conference room between the hours of 7:00 a.m. and 1:00 p.m. on May twenty-first."

Xavier nodded. "That makes sense. You said Iris sent the email at eleven fifty-three."

"Actually, X, we're not sure about that anymore."

"What do you mean?" Xavier's brows knitted.

Tyler consulted the report, although he didn't need to. "The first key-card activity that day occurred at 7:24 a.m."

"Iris arrived early."

"Actually, Iris and I walked in together that morning." In fact, they often arrived at the parking lot at the same time. It was almost as though he subconsciously planned it. Chatting with her in the mornings always put him in a good mood. He tucked those memories away and returned to the cold, hard reality of the key-card access report. "The next activity occurred at 9:32 a.m. Then there was activity at 11:39 a.m. But someone other than Iris entered her office."

Xavier frowned. "Who?"

Tyler looked into his cousin's onyx eyes. "According to the report, X, it was you."

"Thanks for meeting me." Iris settled onto a chair at Cathy's circular kitchen table Tuesday morning.

"Not a problem." Cathy added a plate of chocolate chip cookies to the table. She snatched two before claiming the chair opposite Iris. "Are you sure you don't want me to fix us some lunch? It's almost noon."

In fact, it was only a few minutes past 11:00 a.m. "No, thank you."

"So, what's the latest? You didn't sound

so great on the phone." Cathy bit into a cookie.

"Ty fired me."

The stark words sent Cathy into a coughing fit. Her graphic designer friend struggled to catch her breath. "What? Why?"

"He thinks I'm the one who leaked the test results to *The Gamer's Seat*." Iris absently stirred sweetener into her coffee mug.

"What in the hell would make him think that?" Cathy's perfect complexion glowed almost as red as the scarlet scarf accessorizing her black blouse and matching crew pants. Her feet were bare, exposing the black polish accenting her toenails.

"Whoever sent the test results to *The Gamer's Seat* used my computer and Anderson Adventures email account."

"Pete Kimball." Cathy gritted the competitor's name.

Iris sipped her coffee as she mulled that over. "This isn't him."

"What makes you so sure?"

"When I confronted him this morning, he seemed genuinely surprised." Iris recalled the shock and confusion in Peter's eyes. "Besides, employees need a key card with a special code to get into the offices on the executive floor. I don't think he'd have contacts with that kind of access."

"Are executives the only ones with the special key cards?" There was dread in Cathy's question.

"That's right."

Cathy's dark eyes widened. "One of Anderson Adventures' executives framed you?"

"It seems like it."

Her cookies forgotten, Cathy stared at Iris. "Holy cow. Who have you pissed off?"

"I don't know." Iris stared blindly across Cathy's little kitchen and through her sliding glass doors. "I didn't have enough interaction with anyone to piss them off."

"Does anyone feel threatened by you?"

"I don't think so. Why would they?" Iris pictured the company's executives, as well as their associates. Tyler was the only person with whom she'd ever had a tense exchange, and that was only because he refused to see reason. "Anderson Adventures is a very healthy environment. I never sensed any competition between departments or hostilities between associates."

Silence settled between them as Iris again struggled with the enormous strain of her circumstances. How had she ended up in this situation again? What made her such an easy target for corporate shenanigans? She had to clear her name. But how? Iris spent more time glowering into her mug than actually drinking her coffee. She gazed absently around the room.

Cathy's kitchen was a confusing rainbow of vibrant hues: sunset-orange walls and lemon-yellow curtains. Her countertop and flooring were olive green. Her appliances were brilliant white. The result was a room bursting with a joyful cacophony of colors. It made it difficult to brood. She finished her coffee.

"What are you going to tell your sisters?" Cathy's question added to Iris's anxiety.

"I'd like to tell them as little as possible but we don't keep secrets from each other." Iris collected her mug and Cathy's, then rose to pour them both another cup from the coffeemaker on the counter.

"Just remember, this was never your fault." Cathy held Iris's gaze as she returned with their coffee. "Someone set you up. We need to figure out who did it and why?"

"And what the heck am I going to do about it?" Iris returned to her seat. "I have no idea how I'm going to clear my name."

"You have to convince Ty that someone is framing you."

"How do I do that? He won't listen to me. He's convinced I'm the leak."

"Give him a day or two to calm down, then try again."

Iris exhaled a deep breath and lowered her head to fight back hot tears of anger. "Do you know the worst part?"

"What?"

Iris swallowed twice to dislodge the lump in her throat. "He told me he trusted me. And I believed him."

Cathy leaned closer and put a comforting hand on her shoulder. "Iris . . . did you sleep with him?"

Iris hesitated. "Yes."

Their nights together had been precious and wonderful. They'd revealed themselves to each other in more than a physical way. Their loving had been generous and caring. They'd been vulnerable to each other because they'd had trust. Or so she'd thought. The sharing had been beautiful. Now those memories turned her stomach. How could she have been such a fool? Worse than that: How could she have given him her heart?

Cathy squeezed Iris's shoulder. "For his sake, that's one secret I recommend you keep from your sisters."

Tyler waited for his cousin to respond to his announcement that Xavier's key card had been used to enter Iris's office.

"That's impossible." Xavier sounded baffled. "I haven't used my key card in that door since Iris has been here. Are you sure it's my card?"

Tyler read the key-card number from the report.

Xavier followed along, reading the back of his card, which hung from a belt loop at his hip. "That's my number. But I swear I haven't used my card on that door in months."

"Could someone else have used your card?"

"No, I —" Xavier stopped himself. His dark eyes clouded with confusion. "But she wouldn't . . ."

"Who?" Tyler's patience was at an all-time low. He'd just accused the woman he was falling in love with of betraying him and his company. He didn't think he'd ever done anything more difficult or more painful. It had been like tearing his heart from his chest without anesthesia. Now it was possible he'd been wrong all along.

Xavier's dark eyes were troubled. "Lauren needed to use the restroom. But she didn't want to wait for Sherry to buzz her back into our offices so I loaned her my key card."

Tyler took a figurative punch to his solar

plexus. Did this explain the leak from Iris's computer?

"You loaned your security card to Lauren?" Tyler's voice sounded grim to his ears. "She doesn't even work here."

"I know." Regret was heavy in Xavier's voice. But it was too late. The game was already in play. "I wasn't thinking."

"It's against company policy to let other people use your key card." Why couldn't the nontechnical people in their company wrap their minds around the critical reason for this policy: security?

Xavier scrubbed his hands over his face. "We don't know that Lauren used my card to get into Iris's office."

"Did you access Iris's office?"

"No, but . . . it never occurred to me that she would use my card to sneak around the company."

"That's why the security policy exists. It takes away even the possibility of someone using another person's key card for stuff like this." Tyler tamped down on his anger. He wasn't here to beat up on Xavier. He was after the truth.

Xavier rose and paced to his office window. He spoke over his shoulder. "You think Lauren used my key card to get into Iris's office and send the email to *The*

Gamer's Seat?"

"Why else would your key card show up on the report the day the email was sent to Tipper?"

"But Lauren doesn't have Iris's computer password."

Tyler rubbed the back of his neck. "Unfortunately, Iris doesn't always lock her computer before leaving her office." He knew this. He'd been in her office when she'd forgotten and he'd had to remind her. Why hadn't he listened to her when she'd tried to tell him that earlier? Because he'd put Anderson Adventures' needs first.

Xavier looked over his shoulder. "Another person who doesn't follow the security rules. We must drive you nuts."

"Yes, you do."

Xavier turned back to the window. "This is hard to accept."

"Believe me, I know how you feel."

"I trusted her. Why would she leak confidential information about our company to the press?"

"Ask her." Tyler had wondered the same thing about Iris when he thought she'd tried to sabotage the company. Now it seemed she'd been set up.

I'm asking you to believe me. Trust me, Ty.

Tyler heard Iris's words again and was sick

to his stomach. He should have listened to her. He should have trusted her.

Xavier checked his watch. "Lauren's meeting me for lunch in about an hour."

"All right."

"What do I do if she admits to everything — taking the test results, using my card to gain access to Iris's office, sending the email to *The Gamer's Seat*?" Xavier faced Tyler.

Tyler's temper stirred. "We could have her arrested and charged with the federal crimes of leaking trade secrets and confidential company information."

He'd threatened Iris with those charges. His heart twisted in his chest.

Xavier crossed back to sit at his desk. "How could I have been so stupid?" He held his head in his hands.

They'd both been stupid. Xavier had trusted a woman who'd betrayed them. Tyler had accused a woman he should have believed in.

"I'd rather avoid the negative publicity of having Lauren arrested."

Xavier lowered his hands. "I agree."

"But for the sake of the company, she has to be banned from our offices."

Xavier met Tyler's gaze. "How hard was it for you to confront Iris?"

"Extremely." Tyler rose from his seat. "I'll

let you get ready. In the meantime, I'll send a company-wide reminder that no one is to loan their key card to anyone. Ever."

"Ty." Xavier's voice brought Tyler to a stop. "I'm sorry for the trouble this has caused you and Iris. Frankly, I like her. It was hard to believe she could have been the leak."

"As it turns out, she wasn't." Tyler shoved his fists into the front pockets of his gray Dockers. "I should have followed my instincts and asked for the key-card access report sooner."

Iris had asked him to trust her. He hadn't, not at first. When he asked for her forgiveness, would she be as unrelenting? What could he do to make things right between them?

Chapter 14

Iris hesitated in the doorway to Tyler's office Wednesday morning. She ignored the way his ice-blue button-down shirt spread across the width of his broad shoulders. He rose from his seat at his small conversation table and crossed to her. Iris looked away from his lean hips and long, powerful legs clothed in granite-gray Dockers.

"Iris, thank you for coming." Tyler pushed the doorstop free with the toe of his black loafer, allowing his door to close, then gestured toward the table. "Please have a seat."

Her heart pounded against her chest. Judging by Tyler's tense expression, he wasn't looking forward to this meeting, either. *Then why am I here? Are they planning to sue me? Do I need a lawyer?*

Iris squared her shoulders and strode into the room. She sat at the table, setting her briefcase on the floor beside her, then folded her hands on the Plexiglas surface. She channeled her inner Rose. *Don't show weakness.*

"What's this about?" Hopefully her voice sounded more forceful in reality than it did in her head.

Tyler joined her at the table and took his sweet time answering. It was a test of her self-restraint to remain still under his intense regard.

Finally, he broke his silence. "I wanted to formally apologize for accusing you of leaking the test results. Further investigation proved that you weren't involved."

"Then who was?" Iris's heart rose to her throat. *What is Tyler saying? Has my name been cleared?*

"Lauren. She used Xavier's key card to enter your office. She must have been able to get into your email account because you hadn't locked your system."

Lauren? Iris hadn't been expecting that. "How do you know it was Lauren?"

"She admitted to everything." Tyler shook his head as though in disbelief or denial. "Taking Xavier's copy of the failed test results, using Xavier's card to access your office and sending the email from your account."

The extent of Lauren's deception stole

Iris's breath. Was this really happening — or had someone cast her as a secondary heroine in a prime-time soap opera without her permission? "Why would she do that?"

Tyler rubbed the back of his neck. "She wanted to make me look incompetent so that my father would name Xavier CEO of Anderson Adventures instead of me."

A flash of hot, stinging rage shot through Iris's system. "That evil witch."

"Agreed." Tyler's voice was grim. "Her ambition caused a lot of damage, some of it possibly irreparable."

"No wonder your aunt doesn't like her."

"What makes you think Aunt Kayla doesn't like Lauren?"

Iris surprised herself with a burst of laughter. It eased the frown from her expression and startled Tyler. "Do you really think your aunt can't remember Lauren's name or what she does for a living? Of course she can. But pretending to forget is a mother's way of telling her adult son that she doesn't approve of his girlfriend."

"That sounds like something Aunt Kayla would do." Tyler's face eased into a warm grin that stopped Iris's heart.

She pulled her gaze from Tyler's lips and focused instead on her hands. They were folded in a white-knuckled grip on the table.

Iris made herself relax. "Xavier must be devastated. He'd trusted Lauren."

Equally as devastating as learning the person you love doesn't trust you. Iris inhaled sharply at the pain in her chest.

"I'm sure this experience will make it hard for Xavier to trust someone again." Tyler's ebony eyes were clouded with concern.

"I'm glad you were able to get this cleared up."

"I'm sorry it happened. I'm even sorrier for my reaction." Tyler hesitated. "I know my accusation hurt you. I truly regret that. I should have believed in you, Iris. Will you accept my apology?"

Tyler's voice was deep and low. Seductive. Iris struggled under his spell. His dark eyes pleaded with her. She looked away. Deep inside she was angry with him and she wanted to remain that way. But in her heart she knew there wasn't any reason to hold a grudge. Enough people had been hurt by Lauren's selfish aspirations. "Yes, I'll accept your apology."

"Thank you." Tyler gave her another heart-stopping grin. "Would you also be willing to help us complete the campaign launch?"

Iris stiffened. That was a little trickier. "Yes, but I'd prefer to work from home."

She braced herself for an argument. It never came.

"All right." Tyler's words were thick with disappointment.

Iris was disappointed, too, and hurt. She'd begged Tyler to believe her and his response had been an unequivocal no. How could he expect her to work from Anderson Adventures' offices after that? She couldn't work that closely — literally or figuratively — with Tyler any longer. In fact, Iris needed to leave. Now. "If there's nothing else, I have to get back to work."

Tyler's muscles tensed as he watched Iris collect her purse and briefcase. She rose from her seat. She couldn't leave, not yet.

"There's one more thing." He stood on legs that weren't quite steady and circled the table to stand beside her.

"What is it?" She faced him as though they were polite strangers, as though the memories and passions of the past three months had never existed.

His gaze took in her figure-hugging red skirt suit and matching pumps. "Us."

Iris's eyes flared, then narrowed. "There is no us."

Tyler raised both hands, palms out. "Please hear me out."

"I have other clients waiting for me." She

stepped to the side but Tyler blocked her way. His reaction seemed to surprise both of them.

"I'm sorry I accused you of trying to sabotage the company." He couldn't read the expression on her face. Were his words enough? Did she want more?

"You're forgiven." She tried to step around him again.

Again, Tyler mirrored her move, blocking her path. "When we first met, you asked that we be honest with each other. Why did you say you've forgiven me when it's obvious that you haven't?"

Iris fisted her hands on her waist. The heat of her glare threatened to turn him to ashes. "You should have believed in me."

Tyler tamped down on his panic. "I did believe you. If I didn't, I wouldn't have asked for the key-card access report."

"You should have asked for that report before you accused me." She jabbed a finger in his direction. "You accused me of the most vile and disgusting charges. If you knew me, you'd have known I'd never betray your trust."

The pain he'd caused her was in her voice. So were her tears. The realization hurt so much, it stripped him of breath.

"You're right." Tyler struggled to speak.

"Honey, you're right. I should have known. I was thoughtless and rash."

"And stupid."

"And stupid." He knew she was right. "But, honey, if you give me another chance, I promise I won't be stupid again."

"Another chance?" Iris cocked her head. "This isn't the first time you've believed someone else's lies over my word. The first time, you chose to believe Pete Kimball instead of me. And stop calling me honey."

"I didn't know you then."

"Apparently, you don't know me now, either. You were my client. I could never betray you." She lowered her voice. "You were my lover. You said you trusted me."

The heartache in her eyes reflected the pain in his chest. His gaze lifted to her glossy raven tresses. His hand trembled with the memory of their softness against his palm. "What can I do to convince you that I'm sorry?"

"Nothing. There's nothing you can do."

Iris's words nearly dropped him to his knees. They left him without hope. This time when she stepped around him to leave, Tyler didn't get in her way.

"It was Lauren all along." Iris sipped the cup of chai tea Lily had offered her after their Wednesday family dinner. "I should have known."

It was a warm evening in early June. Night was beginning to fall. Lily had a CD of Patti LaBelle's greatest hits playing softly in the background.

"How were you supposed to know?" Rose was the only one eating the key-lime pie Lily had made for dessert.

"She was waiting for me outside my office one day, right before lunch. She told me she thought Xavier would make a better CEO for Anderson Adventures because she thought Ty was incompetent." Iris shook her head with a heavy sigh. "I bet she'd just sent the email minutes before I arrived."

The dining area still carried the savory aroma of the pasta Lily had made for their dinner — oregano, garlic, peppers and onions drifted around the room. As usual, the dinner had been wonderful. Lily was a talented cook. But Iris had been too upset to enjoy the meal.

Rose looked up from her key-lime pie. "Iris, I owe you an apology."

Iris gave Rose a wide-eyed look. "For what?"

"For not believing that you knew what you were doing when you started your firm. And for not believing that you could handle the

Anderson Adventures account."

Iris gave her sister a reluctant smile. "There were days I didn't believe I could handle this account."

Rose shook her head. "But you shoved aside those doubts and persisted despite Kimball's attempt to undermine you, the conflict between Ty and his father, and then this leak. I'm proud of you."

This was one of those moments that Iris had often fantasized about. She blinked back the sting of tears. "Thanks, Rosie. That means a lot."

Lily reached over and squeezed Iris's forearm. "The mystery is solved. The Andersons have dealt with Lauren — poor Xavier. And Tyler apologized to you. Have you forgiven him?"

It was a little harder for Iris to swallow the tea past the lump building in her throat. "I've forgiven him but his lack of faith in me is not something I can forget."

"So what does that mean?" Rose waved her forkful of key-lime pie. "You're breaking up with him before your relationship has even started?"

"What relationship?" Iris snorted. "You can't have a relationship without trust."

"But he does trust you." Lily sounded as

though she was buying whatever Tyler was selling.

"He's said that before." Iris felt a stirring of irritation. "First, he believed Pete Kimball when Kimball told him RGB had fired me for unethical behavior."

"It impressed me that Anderson didn't just take Kimball's word for it." Rose waved her fork again. "He asked for your side of the story rather than letting Kimball slander you."

Iris stared into her empty mug. Rose had a point. "We'd just met. I could understand his not trusting me. But after we'd been working together for three months, he should have known I'd never betray a client."

Lily drank more tea. "The fact that Ty ran the keycard access report proves he believed in you."

Rose shrugged her shoulder. "You're being too hard on him."

Iris stared at her eldest sister in shock. She must have misunderstood Rose. "Are you saying you think I should give Ty another chance?"

Rose shrugged again. "Why not?"

Iris exchanged a look of disbelief with Lily before attempting to answer Rose's question. "You think all men are bad. Why would you tell me to forgive Ty?"

Rose held Iris's gaze. "Because he asked for the keycard access report."

"He should've asked for that report before he told me to leave Anderson Adventures." Iris crossed her arms over her chest. "If he'd had that report, he wouldn't have had to fire me."

Rose actually laughed. "You're going to hold a grudge because he ran the report *after* instead of *before* he accused you of sending the email? Why can't you just be happy that he asked for it at all?"

Lily gestured toward Rose with her mug of tea. "I agree with Rose."

Rose's wide-eyed stare mocked her. "Shocking."

"I know." Lily smiled. "The fact that Ty asked for the report shows progress."

"I'm still surprised that you're advocating for Ty." Iris stared at Rose, wondering what had changed for her sister. "After Ben, I thought you were convinced all men were evil and not to be trusted."

Rose pushed aside her now-empty dessert plate. "Perhaps I did get a little carried away. Men like Ben aren't to be trusted. However, Ty is not like Ben. He can admit when he's wrong and he can say that he's sorry."

Iris looked from Rose to Lily. Maybe they were right. Still, she hesitated. "What if he hurts me again?"

"We'll break both of his legs." Rose's voice was a growl.

Lily squeezed Iris's forearm again. "The fact is, every relationship comes with risks, Iris. The question you have to ask yourself is whether Ty is worth the risk."

"What does 'worth the risk' mean?" Iris was reluctant to answer that question, even for herself.

"When you're with him, does he make you feel special?" Rose put down her teacup. "When you're away from him, do you feel like a part of you is missing?"

Iris blinked. It was as though Rose had read her mind. "Is that how Ben made you feel?"

"No." Rose gave her a half smile. "Is that how you feel with Ty?"

"Yes." Iris briefly closed her eyes.

"Then he's worth the risk." Lily said the words that were in Iris's mind.

"Fine. You want me to say it, I will." Restless, Iris pushed away from the table and stood to pace the dining room. "I've fallen in love with Ty Anderson. Big deal. He doesn't love me."

"You said he has feelings for you." Lily

watched her with concern in her tawny eyes.

Rose frowned. "Why don't you just ask him?"

"I'm not going to ask him." Iris glared at her elder sister over her shoulder. "All this talk about whether Ty's worth the risk is a waste of time. The fact is you can't have love without trust and he's proven he doesn't trust me."

"Then what *are* you going to do?" Lily asked.

Iris stilled. She gritted her teeth as a burning pain radiated across her chest. *So this is what a broken heart feels like.* "I'm going to learn to live without him."

"This is becoming a habit." Iris's expression was inscrutable as she stared up at Tyler from the threshold of her townhome's front door Thursday evening.

"I'm not giving up on you. On us." Tyler took advantage of her shock to slip past her and into her home.

As she locked her front door, Tyler drank in her appearance as though it had been weeks instead of a day since he'd last seen her. His gaze slid from her slender back clothed in a snow-white jersey to her ruby-red capris. Her bare feet allowed him to enjoy the whimsical sight of the pale pink nail polish accenting her pedicure. Tyler ached to pull Iris into his embrace and lose himself in the closeness his misguided actions had cost him. He'd wronged her. Could she ever forgive him?

Iris's cool coffee eyes tossed out a challenge. "When did you and I become *us*?"

"The moment we started working together." Tyler willed her to remember the chemistry they shared, in and out of bed. "Yes, we've butted heads. We're both strong willed. But we were a great team. We still are."

Iris stalked past Tyler. "So now you want to talk about what a good team we made. Why didn't you remember that when you were accusing me of trying to destroy your company?"

Tyler spoke to her back as he followed her into her living room. "If you want me to apologize again, I will. I'll say it as many times as you want to hear it. Honey, I'm sorry. I was wrong. Please give us another chance."

"Stop calling me honey." Iris threw up her arms as she spun to face him. "Why should I give you another chance? Because you need someone to wrap up your product campaign?"

"If it was only about the launch, I'd call

Pete Kimball."

Anger flashed across Iris's elegant features. "Be careful what you wish for, Ty."

"I'm wishing for you." Tyler stripped himself bare for her. His raw words revealed his vulnerability. "What do I need to do to convince you to forgive me? Tell me and I'll do it. All I want is a second chance with you."

Iris was shaking her head long before Tyler finished speaking. "You still don't get it. I needed you to step out on faith for me, to believe in me despite the evidence. Despite what other people might say. All I wanted was for you to trust me."

"If I didn't trust you, I wouldn't have asked for the report."

"I don't mean trust me in hindsight. If you trusted me, I wouldn't have to defend myself to you, ever, because you'd know me." Iris's coffee eyes were dark with regret, an emotion Tyler had become all too familiar with.

"I *do* know you."

"You do? What do you know?"

Tyler winced. She was right to be angry. But he wasn't leaving until she'd heard everything he had to say. Everything.

"Yes, Iris Beharie, I know you. I know you have guts. You started your own company. I know you're independent. You were annoyed when your sister gave my father your business card." He dared a step toward her. "You're tough. You threatened Tipper with a lawsuit if he claimed that 'Osiris's Journey' wasn't market ready."

Iris's expression remained cool. "So you've noticed a few things. Congratulations. You aren't a complete knucklehead."

"I also know the most important thing of all." Tyler closed the gap between them.

Iris stepped back toward the sofa. "What's that?"

"I know that I'm in love you."

Iris dropped onto the couch. Her eyes widened and her lips parted in shock. She stared up at him in silence.

Tyler's smile shook. "Is it really that surprising?"

Iris remained silent. Had she heard him? Tyler started to repeat himself when she spoke.

"How could you be in love with me when you think I could sabotage your company?"

"I was wrong." Tyler sat beside her and offered her his hand.

Iris's eyes lowered to his open palm before returning to his eyes. "I need you to trust me."

"I do, Iris." Tyler lowered his hand. "Give

me another chance and I'll prove it to you."

Iris stared at her hands folded in her lap for another quiet moment. This time, Tyler waited.

"I can't take that risk. I'm sorry, Ty." She stood and walked to her front door. She held it open as she turned back to Tyler.

No! Tyler's mind shouted denials. He rose slowly. "Iris, I —"

"I'm sorry." But she couldn't meet his eyes.

Tyler's mind spun, searching for better arguments, more persuasions, anything that would convince her to let him stay. He had nothing. He walked to the door on unsteady legs. Every step shredded his heart.

He hesitated when he reached her. "I'm the one who's sorry, Iris."

Walking out the door tore his heart out.

"I'm not ready to take charge of the company." Tyler stood in his father's office Friday morning. Through one of the windows, he stared blindly at the fifth-floor view of downtown Columbus. In the past four months, he'd come full circle. From wanting to prove to Foster that he could be the next chief executive officer of their family-owned company to realizing he didn't have what it took to lead Anderson

Adventures.

"Ty, what are you talking about?" Foster's voice carried from his desk behind Tyler. He sounded baffled. "You've been preparing for this since you were eight years old."

"I know." In childhood dreams, you can do anything. But now it was time to grow up.

"The internal launch was wonderful. Our associates are still talking about it. The external campaign was a great success. Presales are at historic highs."

Both accomplishments were all Iris's doing. Now, she wanted nothing to do with him. " 'Osiris's Journey' will be another bestselling game for us."

"Another bestseller that you designed." Foster paused. In the background, Tyler heard a very brief, faint sigh. "Look at me, Ty. After everything you've accomplished, what makes you think you can't lead the company?"

Reluctantly, Ty faced his father. "You taught me that Anderson Adventures is more than products. It's people. But when the company was threatened, I sacrificed a person to protect it even though everything in me told me I was wrong."

A sudden restlessness — and shame? — drove him from the window. Tyler shoved his fists into the front pockets of his black Dockers and paced across his father's office. The room was wide and bright. Thick burgundy carpeting silenced his footsteps.

"You don't think you can lead the company because of the way you handled the leak?" The concern on Foster's expression eased.

"I never should have accused Iris."

"Why, because she still hasn't forgiven you?"

Tyler shot his father a sharp look. "I shouldn't have accused her because she wasn't responsible. My gut told me that. But instead of following my instincts, I believed a piece of paper." He fisted his hands. If he could, he'd build a time machine and make all of this go away.

"Next time, you'll know to listen to your gut."

"There won't be a next time." When he came to the opposite wall, Tyler turned and retraced his steps.

"I certainly hope not." Foster shifted in his seat to face Tyler. "But in the meantime, I'm convinced you can lead the company and our associates once I step down. Kayla agrees."

Shock froze Tyler's feet in place. "How can you say that?"

"Because you did what I asked you to do and you did it well." Foster straightened on his chair.

"I appreciate your support but you're making a mistake. The way I handled Iris when she was suspected of being the leak shows I don't have good judgment."

"Ty, I would have done exactly what you did."

"Then we both would've been wrong." Tyler rubbed his eyes. "I'm sorry. I didn't mean to snap. But I don't think you would've made the same mistake. You would've listened to your instincts and asked all of the right questions before making a final decision." His father's instincts had helped grow a business that had started at a dining room table and made it into an international success.

"I don't understand you, Ty. You've been telling me you wanted to be CEO since you were a child. Why are you now getting cold feet?"

Tyler massaged the back of his neck. "Because I don't want my poor judgment to ruin this forty-three — soon to be forty-four — year-old company."

"Your concern proves you're not going to make the same mistake again. It also means you're the leader Kayla and I want for the company."

Tyler shook his head. "How did you come to that conclusion?"

His father's gaze locked with Tyler's. "Ty, in life, what matters aren't the mistakes you make but the lessons you learn from them."

"Well, I've learned a lot from this particular mistake." Including the fact that second chances are rare.

"Good. They'll serve you well as you lead the company." Foster's confidence in him increased Tyler's restlessness.

He'd hoped this campaign would end differently. In his mind, he'd seen himself earning the promotion and Iris's love. Now, he didn't have either. "No, Dad, I'm no longer confident I can lead the company."

"Then who can?"

"I don't know." Tyler hadn't expected that question. He should have had that second cup of coffee. "Perhaps you can convince Xavier or Van."

"You know neither of them is interested." Foster leaned forward, picking up the silver Cross pen on his desk and rolling it between his fingers. "And no one wants someone from the outside to lead the company."

"I thought you said an outsider was a possibility?" Tyler scowled.

"I only said that to scare you."

Tyler rubbed his eyes. "Yes, well, it worked."

"I know." Foster's grin was unrepentant. "We want to keep Anderson Adventures in the family."

"But you and everyone else were right when you said I don't have people skills." Tyler paced some more. "Lauren used that weakness to hurt the company."

"But she didn't hurt the company." Foster arched an eyebrow. "So obviously you do have people skills. Ty, you're more ready than you think. Besides I'm not retiring tomorrow. There'll be a transition period."

That was a slight relief. Very slight. "How long of a transition?"

Foster relaxed back onto his chair. "After 'Osiris's Journey' releases, I'll announce that I'm retiring at the end of the year. That gives us six months to prepare."

Tyler considered that. "I don't have a choice, do I?"

"You don't. And you'd regret passing on this opportunity. You know that." Foster shrugged. "I'm retiring, Ty. Not dropping off the face of the earth. You can call me whenever you need advice."

"All right. If you think I'm ready, I'll take over as CEO once you retire." Tyler wandered back to the window. He met

Foster's gaze over his shoulder. "Thank you."

"You can also use the time to make things right with Iris." Foster rose from his desk and approached Tyler. "If you love her, son, don't give up."

Tyler looked out the window again. The vivid blue sky and glass-and-metal buildings were invisible to him. Instead he saw wide, sad eyes the color of strong coffee. "I've hurt her too badly. She's not interested in anything more I have to say. And frankly, I can't think of anything else to express how very sorry I am."

"Then don't say anything." Foster's hand came to rest on Tyler's shoulder. "Actions speak louder."

Finally, a glimmer of hope. "Are you suggesting I buy her flowers or candy?"

Foster shook his head. "Those things would be nice. But I think, in this case, you need a more personal gesture."

Tyler's frustration returned. "Like what?"

Foster patted his shoulder. "You'll think of something, son."

Iris's agency phone rang Monday evening, breaking her concentration from the media pitch she was writing for "Osiris's Journey." She saved the file, lowered the volume on her CD player and picked up the receiver.

"This is Iris Beharie. May I help you?"

"Ms. Beharie, this is Cooper Johnson with Central City Medical Health." The voice on the other end of the line was all business.

Cooper Johnson was a familiar name. If memory served, he was the vice president of marketing for a major health insurance company.

"Good evening, Mr. Johnson. What can I do for you?" *Please let him ask me for a bid proposal.*

"CCMH is rolling out a new insurance product. I'm sorry to contact you so late in the day but are you available to meet with us in the morning? We'd like your help with our internal and external product launch." Cooper's voice slowed as though he was consulting his calendar.

Yes! Iris's pulse kicked up with excitement over a potential new client with a big project. There was just one challenge. Her eyes drifted to the clock on her computer. It was almost 6:00 p.m. "Mr. Johnson, I'd love to meet with you tomorrow but that doesn't give me time to put together a bid proposal. Could we meet —"

"You misunderstand, Ms. Beharie," Cooper smoothly interrupted. "We aren't requesting a bid proposal. We're awarding you the job. Tomorrow's meeting will provide you with the information you need to put together a budget estimate and a project schedule. Is that acceptable?"

Central City Medical Health was hiring her for a major project? And they didn't want a proposal or references? "You're hiring me?"

"You were highly recommended."

Iris smiled. "By whom?" *Has Lily been passing out my business cards again?*

"Ty Anderson. He staked his reputation that you'd deliver a successful product launch, on time and within budget."

Iris froze. She tried several times to speak. "Ty?"

"Anderson Adventures is a well-respected company." Cooper chuckled. "If Ty's willing to stake his reputation on your work, why should I waste time asking for multiple bids? I was going to contact Kimball & Associates, but Ty told me in great detail about the media exposure, presales and social media success his company garnered from your campaigns."

Iris was overwhelmed. Her heart was beating in her throat. Was this really happening for her? She stuttered her way through a reply. "Well, uh . . . it was a . . . a team effort."

"He said you'd say that." Cooper chuckled again. "Are you available tomorrow morning?"

"Yes, I'm available." Iris grabbed a pencil and her writing tablet. "Let me take your information."

A little more than an hour later, Iris rang the doorbell of Tyler's colonial-style home. It didn't take him long to answer. He stood in the doorway dressed in baggy gray shorts and a tight black short-sleeved T-shirt. His feet were bare.

"You've shown up at my townhome so many times." Iris tried for light banter. "I thought turnabout would be fair play."

"What are you doing here?" Tyler stepped aside to let her in.

Iris's curious gaze took in his entryway. It was dominated by the polished cherrywood used for the threshold, flooring and trim circling the ceiling. Iris enjoyed the effect. "I wanted to thank you."

"For what?" Tyler led her down a short, narrow hallway to a silver-and-black sitting room.

Iris gratefully sank onto the love seat. Her legs weren't going to support her much longer. "Cooper Johnson called me this evening. Did you put him up to it?"

"Why would I do that?" Tyler leaned against the wall on the opposite side of the room. His arms were crossed over his impressive chest and his eyes were fixed on her. "I know you don't want people to help you."

Iris took in the framed abstract paintings hanging on the walls. Personal photos and whimsical sculptures kept the room's decor from being cold. Her gaze dropped to the hardwood flooring beneath her sneakered feet. "He told me you'd staked your reputation on my being able to produce a successful product launches for CCMH."

Tyler's initial reaction was a short, sharp obscenity. "Coop has a big mouth."

Iris lifted her head and looked him in the eyes. "You're taking a great risk, tying my reputation to yours. If I fail, we're both going down."

"You're not going to fail."

"How do you know that?"

"I know you." Tyler looked away. "You're thorough, well organized and creative. And like me, you love a challenge."

Iris stood and walked to him. "You're trusting me with your reputation. Why?" She stopped less than an arm's length from him. She couldn't read the expression in his eyes. But she sensed his body stiffen. Was he as afraid as she was?

Tyler straightened from the wall and lowered his arms. "Things didn't work out for us personally but I believe in you, Iris." His voice was gruff. "You're good at what you do. I want you to be happy."

Iris blinked back her tears. She took his large, strong hands in hers. The feel of his warm skin sent a flash of pleasure up her arms. "Ty, I've been falling in love with you since you made that joke about being my Prince Charming. All I needed was to know that you trust me. Now I do."

His smile brightened his face and warmed her heart. The shutters lifted from his ebony eyes. In their dark depths, she saw how deeply he loved her. Tyler drew her to him and kissed her, long, hard and deep. She tasted how much he'd missed her. She'd missed him just as much. He held her tightly to his long lean muscles. Iris rose up on her toes to mold her body more closely to his. She wrapped her arms around his broad shoulders. Tyler's tongue slipped between her lips. She drew it deeper into her mouth. His erection pressed against her abdomen.

Tyler lifted his head. "I've missed you." His voice was low. The words reverberated in her heart. "I'm lost without you."

"I've been so empty without you," Iris whispered back.

"I have a favorite song now."

"What is it?" She smiled up at him.

"It's the sound of you walking back into my life." Tyler lowered his head and kissed her senseless again.

ABOUT THE AUTHOR

Regina Hart is the contemporary romance pseudonym of award-winning author Patricia Sargeant. Her various pastimes and hobbies include sports — both college and pros — movies, music and, of course, reading. She loves chatting with readers. Contact her at BooksbyPatricia@yahoo.com. You can also friend her on Facebook as Patricia Sargeant / Regina Hart.